In the
Shadow
of the Alamo

In the
Shadow
of the Alamo

SHERRY GARLAND

GULLIVER BOOKS

HARCOURT, INC.

San Diego   New York   London

To Aunt Velma (1903–2001)—
With loving memories of my first trip to Mexico

www.harcourt.com

Gulliver Books is a trademark of Harcourt, Inc., registered in the
United States of America and/or other jurisdictions.

Library of Congress Cataloging-in-Publication Data
Garland, Sherry.
In the shadow of the Alamo/Sherry Garland.
p.   cm.
(Gulliver Great Episodes.)
Summary: Conscripted into the Mexican army,
fifteen-year-old Lorenzo Bonifacio makes some unexpected
alliances and learns some harsh truths about General Santa Anna
as the troops move toward the Battle of the Alamo.
1. Mexico—History—1821–1861—Juvenile fiction.
[1. Mexico—History—1821–1861—Fiction.   2. Alamo (San Antonio, Tex.)—
Siege, 1836—Fiction.   3. Soldiers—Fiction.   4. Santa Anna, Antonio Lâopez
de, 1794?–1876—Fiction.   5. War—Fiction.]   I. Title.
PZ7.G18415Ip 2001
[Fic]—dc21   2001000695
ISBN 0-15-201744-5

Text set in Meridien
Display set in Memphis
Designed by Cathy Riggs

First edition
A C E G H F D B

Printed in the United States of America

ACKNOWLEDGMENTS

With any historical novel, research is the backbone of the story. I would like to give special thanks to Kevin Young for sharing his expertise about the Mexican army, especially its uniforms and weapons. *Muchas gracias* go to Tony Garcia for giving me insight into the Mexican culture (*¡Viva Zapata!*), and to Julia Mercedes Castilla for her help with Spanish words. As always, I take total responsibility for any errors. And finally, deepest thanks to my ever patient husband, who never complains when I drag him to remote and strange places in the name of research.

The list of reference sources I consulted for this book is too long to enumerate, but I would like to acknowledge a few of the ones that I found to be valuable and also accessible to the general public. First and foremost was *With Santa Anna in Texas: A Personal Narrative of the Revolution* by

José Enrique de la Peña, translated and edited by Carmen Perry. Other useful sources include *The Mexican National Army, 1822–1852* by William A. DePalo, Jr.; *Life in Mexico* by Frances Calderón de la Barca; *The Alamo: An Illustrated History* by George Nelson; *Texian Iliad: A Military History of the Texas Revolution, 1835–1836* by Stephen L. Hardin; *The Alamo and the War of Texan Independence 1835–36 (Men-at-Arms Series, 173)* by Philip Haythornthwaite, illustrated by Paul Hannon; *The Alamo Remembered: Tejano Accounts and Perspectives* by Timothy M. Matovina; *Eyewitness to the Alamo* by Bill Groneman; *A Time to Stand* by Walter Lord; *100 Days in Texas: The Alamo Letters* by Wallace O. Chariton; and *Duel of Eagles: The Mexican and U.S. Fight for the Alamo* by Jeff Long.

ONE

■ ■ ■

Los Soldados

If someone sat me down on a big rock this very day and asked me: "Lorenzo Bonifacio, exactly how did you end up a soldier in General Santa Anna's army, hundreds of leagues from your tiny village in northern Guanajuato state?" I suppose my first answer would have to be: "It is because of Catalina, the goatherd."

It happened a year ago, in early November. Candle wax and marigolds left over from *el día de los muertos*, the Day of the Dead, which had been celebrated the day before, still clung to graves. I was minding my own affairs, working away in the *maguey* fields alongside every other able-bodied man in our village, cutting the fat, fleshy leaves with my machete and siphoning the sweet yellow sap that would be fermented into *pulque*, a drink so strong it curls your toes. The few extra *reales* we earned from harvesting the wild *maguey* were often the difference between a full belly and starvation over the winter. I was feeling very good that day for the sky was clear and glorious, and the distant Sierra Madres shimmered like purple jewels. Their crests were tipped with snow and the thought that the blistering hot weather was ending sent a thrill through my innocent heart.

It was early afternoon. We had already broken for *la comida* and eaten our meager meals of *tortillas* and *frijoles*, and it was time to curl up in whatever shade we could find and take *la siesta*. I knew a secret spot where I could get away from the others—a little nook between two large boulders that caught a good breeze. Sometimes there was a rattlesnake or a Gila monster hiding there, but that never bothered me. I would just scrape the creature aside and sleep snugly away from the snoring of the other workers.

If I had only gone to that secret place to eat the beans, I would not be telling this story today. But Catalina, the goatherd, spoiled my plans. She came running to the field, her plump figure swathed in layers of colored petticoats and skirts, a white blouse, and a bright striped *rebozo* around her shoulders. You would think it was freezing cold, but that is the way she dressed all the time.

I always knew when Catalina was near because I would hear the tap of her long cedar staff, followed by the bleating of a dozen goats and the clanking of the lead goat's bell. Not to mention the smell. And then there was her incessant chatter and giggling. Why she chose me as the object of her affection I have no idea. I am certainly not the most handsome boy in the village, nor the smartest, and by all means I am not the most fortunate. In fact, I am renowned for my bad luck because when I was small a jealous old woman gave me the *mal de ojo*— the evil eye. But no one dared say that to Catalina, else she would clap the offender with her staff. That could be deadly. I have seen Catalina lift a fifty-pound goat with ease. Who knows what muscles lay hidden under those layers of cotton?

I groaned when I saw her coming, for she was a nuisance like a cactus needle under a sandal strap. I tried to hide, but she saw me and shouted.

"Lorenzo! Come quickly! I have something amazing to show you."

It was with great reluctance that I gave in to her call and walked to her side.

"Don't you know it is *siesta* time?" I said in not very kind tones.

"Of course, I know. I did not want to interrupt your work," she replied in a very serious voice.

"Work I do not mind you interrupting," I told her. "But *siesta*—now that is a man's time for himself."

Catalina merely frowned and tapped her cedar pole impatiently. "I thought you would want to know this. I have seen another vision, Lorenzo. A vision of the Virgin of Guadalupe." She closed her eyes and made the sign of the cross.

A normal man might have dropped his water gourd and gone running to see this vision, but I knew Catalina too well. In her lifetime she had seen visions of Our Lady of Guadalupe three times; San Javier, for whom our village is named, twice; her dead mother's face in a mushroom once; and her dead grandmother's face in a pile of bat *guano*. But each time when others had run to see the vision, it was gone. These visions had made her a most unpopular girl, but she was sincere. I would never scoff at poor Catalina ... yet I truly did not want to miss my *siesta*.

With a great sigh, I followed Catalina, knowing it was pointless to refuse. Arguing with her was like butting heads with a billy goat: She always won her little battles of will. Arguing would only prolong the time I had to spend with her. If I looked quickly at whatever mushroom or cactus or rock she wanted, I would have at least some time for my rest.

I followed her to a deep *barranco* where once, long before I was born, water had flowed in great torrents. Now the dry ravine only filled with water after a sudden rain. Generations of trees had lived and died in the dry, rocky bottom. Catalina worked her way through briers and weeds toward a dead willow tree. Its blackened trunk had been split in two by lightning.

"There," she said, pointing to the jagged, broken trunk. "There is where I saw Our Lady of Guadalupe's face. Do you not see her in the tree rings?"

4

I stared at the trunk, squinting my eyes. The goats nibbled at the bark with great interest. I asked myself: *Should I lie to her and tell her I see the Virgin, and hope that she will let me get back to my* siesta? *Or should I tell her no, I do not see anything, and take a chance that she will argue for an hour?* I struggled with my dilemma for several seconds before finally sighing.

"No, Catalina, I do not see it. You are imagining things again." Sometimes I wish I were not such an honest man, but that is the way my dear mother raised me, and I cannot change. Saints above know I've tried. After climbing back up the ravine, I hurried toward my secret hideaway.

Just as I had dreaded, Catalina ran after me, using all her powers of persuasion. One of the goats nibbled at my *sarape,* and I swatted at the animal. "Just leave me alone, Catalina. And get these goats away." I am a very unpleasant person when I do not get enough sleep, and my eyes were getting heavy as stones.

While we were standing there arguing, I suddenly heard shouting and the sound of pounding hooves. We both turned and saw a row of mounted soldiers thundering down upon us. The other farmers, most of them wakened from their sleep, struggled to their feet in terror, cursing and shouting.

"*¡Los soldados!*" Catalina shrieked.

Let me tell you, in Mexico there is only one reason soldiers come to a village as remote as mine. And only

5

one reason they charge into a *maguey* field full of workingmen. Some nations would call it barbaric; we call it bad luck, or fate. The government calls it *la leva*—the levy. Call it what you will, they'd come to conscript us into the army.

The farmers scattered like a flock of startled crows. It may look shameless, but believe me, it is not considered cowardly to run from *la leva,* for to be drafted as a private into the Mexican army is to suffer ten long years of hunger and unbearable living conditions, and quite often it results in death. And all this for a salary so meager it does not buy beans. Thank God I am not a full-blooded Indian. Those poor souls are forced to slave in the army for no pay at all.

So, without another thought, I began running toward the clump of boulders where I knew I could find a good place to hide. But the goats trotted alongside me as if it were a game, and as fate would have it, the lead nanny got in my way and I fell on my face in the dirt. I tried to stand up but lost my balance. The delay was long enough for a dragoon to lasso my shoulders and pull tight. As he dragged me across the field, rocks and cactus cut into my back, my legs, and my poor, unfortunate behind. Now I know what it feels like to be a coyote caught in a trap. For several seconds I fought like a demon, until at last I struggled to my feet and stood like a man. If I had my way, at that moment a certain nanny goat would have been roasting over an open spit.

Catalina shrieked and wept hysterically as she tugged at my sleeve and pounded the soldier's leg with her cedar staff. The dragoon kicked at her with his dirty boot, but the blow only thudded against the layers of clothing. She shouted curses, then threatened to tell her grandfather, a shriveled old man who always smells like tobacco, goats, and pig's urine. He fought with General Guerrero in the Revolution, and though that was twenty years ago he still acts as if he has importance in the military.

The dragoon only laughed as he grabbed Catalina by her long braid and slung her away. I knew there was nothing to be done. Heaven above had decided that I, a fifteen-year-old peasant, whose only desire that day was to slurp a good bowl of hot *caldo* with *tortillas* and afterward have a sweet rest, was to be inducted into the army of His Excellency, Presidente-General Antonio López de Santa Anna.

All this did not surprise me. I have always been an unlucky boy. Besides, the same fate had fallen upon my own father nine years ago when the last levy came to our village. I remember seeing Papa walking in a line with other village men, all taken away like bulls being led to the slaughter. Papa had accepted his fate and had stood tall and handsome. I do not know what war he fought in—there have been too many wars and revolts to keep up with. I do not know who was president then. All I know is that Papa never returned.

So I was to be a soldier, too. So be it. I was not frightened. No, my greatest worry was for my two younger sisters, Dulcinea and Aracelia. Our mother had died from a broken heart and exhaustion three years ago. Without a man in our little adobe hut to help with the work, how would they survive? Such were the thoughts of every man who had a family. But I'm sure these things were the last concern of His Excellency, General Santa Anna.

TWO

■ ■ ■

A Terrible Mistake

While the dragoons tied our hands behind our backs and tethered our feet together so that our steps were like those of a child's, Catalina raced to the village, the goats bleating and jingling as they ran behind her.

In a few moments the church bell rang out deliriously. No doubt at first the priest and the *alcalde*, who rules the village, had refused to believe the simple goatherd. After all, like her goatherd mother before her, Catalina does have a reputation for exaggeration. Then, perhaps they squinted and saw the line of blue soldiers. I imagined the priest falling on his knees in front of the statues of Jesus and Mary, his hands clasped as he prayed for our souls. I knew the wives of the married men would be frantic, trying to console sobbing children.

The thought of sobbing children made my heart sick. What would happen to my dear little sisters, already orphans at the tender ages of nine and eleven? Our only relative now was a widowed aunt, Florencia, a *curendera* devoted to her work. How could she care for two young girls when she was so often caring for the sick of the village, or in the mountains gathering medicinal herbs?

A sudden pain in my wrists interrupted my thoughts. I watched the leader of the conscription party, a sturdy man whose worn blue-and-red uniform seemed to be a size too small for his barrel chest and plump stomach. I heard the soldiers call him Sergeant Ildefonso. He walked down the line of miserable farmers to check each man's tether. When he reached me, he cocked his head to one side.

"How old are you, *muchacho*?" the sergeant asked.

"Fifteen," I replied. Surely he would see the terrible mistake that had been made and set me free. But he merely grunted, loosened my bonds a bit, then moved on to the next man.

The dragoons marched us like captured cattle back to the village of San Javier. All we were lacking was a sizzling brand on our rumps.

When we arrived at the dusty plaza in the middle of the village, it was just as I had expected. Wailing women wrung their hands and pleaded with the sergeant to set their men free.

"*Por favor, el sargento*, we have seven small children. Without my husband, we will all starve to death."

"*Por favor, el sargento,* I am very old and sickly. Do not take my only son."

"*Por favor, el sargento,* I have no mother. If you take Papa, I will be an orphan with no one to care for me."

On and on the pleas filled the air. I saw my aunt Florencia in a corner, her eyes wild as she held my little sisters close to her black skirt. She was the only woman in town who wore black all year round. It was in honor of her bridegroom, who, on their wedding night twenty-five years ago, had died a terrible death at the hands of the Spanish during the Revolution. Not long after that, she witnessed the Spaniards putting the heads of beloved Father Hidalgo and three of his lieutenants in cages and hanging them on hooks in the town of Guanajuato, where she lived. Everyone says the event snapped Aunt Florencia's mind. Consumed with a hatred for the Spanish, she joined the Revolution and fought like a man until Mexico won its independence from Spain.

Aunt Florencia never married again. She took care of my grandparents until they died. The past fifteen years she had dedicated herself to learning the healing skills of a *curendera.* Living in a little hut by herself, she often worked long into the night, making herbal concoctions, burning magical candles, sending up prayers and, some people say, curses. Everyone in the village had used her services at one time or another, much to the dismay of the priest, Father Martín. The respect she commanded was surpassed only by the fear she induced.

As we stood in the plaza, the raucous crowd became so loud that the dogs began barking. Finally the sergeant shouted, *"¡Silencio!"* He removed an ancient-looking *pistola* from his belt and fired into the air, over the top of the church belfry. The roar made the women shrink back and grow silent. Small children began to whimper.

"Señoras, I do not have the power to set your husbands free," the sergeant said, as he replaced the pistol. "The commander, Lieutenant Ochoa, will be here shortly. He will hear all your excuses and select the men needed to fill the levy quota. In the meantime, go prepare food and drink for these weary soldiers who fight for Mexico's freedom. We have not eaten all day."

The *alcalde* had changed into black trousers, a dark coat, and a wide red sash, which he wore around his waist. He had pinned three medals of honor on his chest. He wore these only on official occasions. Turning to the women, the *alcalde* said, "You heard *el sargento.* Go, quickly!" The *alcalde* clapped his hands. The women darted away like a covey of quails.

A sickening feeling overcame me as I slumped on the steps of the church portico beside the other captured men. Obviously the *alcalde* was helpless to do anything against armed dragoons.

Father Martín had also changed into his best frock and new sandals, and had combed his white hair. He walked among the tethered men, saying a prayer for each. When he came to me, he knelt down.

"Lorenzo Bonifacio, why are you here? You are only a boy."

I shrugged. "It is the bad luck of the Bonifacio family we have talked about so often, *Padre*. The evil eye—"

"Posh!" He waved his hand. "I have told you there is no such thing as the evil eye." He smiled. "The quota for the levy is supposed to be filled with conscripts between the ages of sixteen and fifty. I am sure that the lieutenant will let you go when he arrives. Be patient, my son." He mumbled a quick prayer, blessed me, and moved on.

In a moment Catalina shuffled over to the covered portico, dragging a heavy wooden bucket filled with cool water from the communal well. She dipped a gourd into the pail and put it to my parched lips. I slurped the liquid down noisily, spilling half on my dirt-covered shirt. I did not care; it felt wonderfully cool.

"*Muchas gracias*," I said, noticing that her dirty face was streaked with tears.

"It isn't fair, Lorenzo," she said, blotting the water on my chin with the corner of her striped *rebozo*. "You are a good person."

I shrugged. "Ah, and do you think that only bad men are conscripted into the army?"

She pondered the question a moment. "Well, it should be that way. A good person would not shoot a musket and kill another, would he?"

"He might, if he was being shot at himself."

Catalina pouted her lips, making deep dimples show in her plump cheeks. She dipped the *rebozo* into the bucket and gently wiped dirt from my face. Who would think that a goatherd would know such tenderness?

"In my opinion, the generals should only take wicked men, like those in the jails," she said. "Or at least men who have no families."

"I will tell General Santa Anna your opinion when I see him. I am sure he will agree." I shook my head. It was always such with girls. They say they have no stomach for killing, but they wring the necks of chickens and slaughter goats without a second thought.

"But how can you stand to leave our village? It is all you have ever known."

I shrugged. "Who knows, maybe I will get to see a big town with grand buildings and beautiful gardens and beautiful women. Maybe I am tired of this little village with its dirty streets. Maybe I am tired of talking to girls who smell like goats."

Before Catalina could respond, the other men began loudly complaining that they wanted water, too, so she moved on, a deep frown on her face.

We did not have long to wait for the commander to arrive. Lieutenant Ochoa rode into the village on a beautiful black horse. His silver spurs and the silver ornaments on his saddle twinkled in the sunlight. He was a small, trim young man, almost dainty in appearance, with the exception of a large, round head that looked very much like a pumpkin. When he smiled, he showed pointy little teeth. While the other soldiers had a thick layer of dust on their faded blue coats and pants and black boots, the lieutenant showed not a speck of dirt on his bright new blue-and-red uniform. The breeze softly rustled the plume of feathers on the tall, stiff *shako* strapped to his head.

Like many officers in the Mexican army, the lieutenant was a *criollo;* his light skin was the badge of pure Spanish descent. In such a system, it is not always the talent of a man that gets him promotions but the color of his skin and the name of his father. I could easily imagine the lieutenant sitting behind a government desk in Mexico City or making intricate turns in a delicate dance or penning poetry beneath a tree, but I could not imagine him in the heat of battle splattered with blood.

To my surprise, beside the lieutenant rode Esteban Esquivel, the son of Don Carlos Esquivel, the wealthiest *hacienda* owner in our part of the region. Esteban rode a dappled gray Andalusian mare, whose white mane and tail shimmered in the sunlight like corn silk. Behind him came an Indian servant driving a clumsy *carreta* pulled by two good oxen and half filled with provisions.

At the sight of such an important person as Esteban Esquivel, a ripple of hope passed over the conscripts. If anyone could save us, it was the Esquivel family. The Esquivels had made their fortune supplying corn and beef to the silver mines near Guanajuato. During the Revolution, many mines closed down and the Esquivels fell on hard times. Still, they were more powerful and more wealthy than any man in our village could ever hope to be.

Don Carlos Esquivel owned much of the land on which we farmed. As payment we gave him a portion of the harvest. In addition to cash crops like corn and cotton and beans, each family grew just enough vegetables to keep itself alive. A few chickens for eggs and a goat for milk made a man a king. Most farmers took out loans from Don Carlos to buy farming tools and animals that pulled the plow, or for the large two-wheeled *carretas*. It was an accepted fact that most of us would never be able to repay the loans and get ahead in life. Even so, I am told that slaving in the cornfields is better than being a miner, like my grandfathers, who died from the strain of working night and day in the belly of the earth, carrying hundreds of pounds of ore on their bare backs and breathing foul air.

Don Carlos had two lovely daughters, both married to wealthy landowners, and one son, Esteban, three years older than I. I had seen Esteban at the annual *herraderos*, the roundup and branding of the cattle, and at an occasional bullfight during a festival. At such events all of the farmers and nearby Indians would go to the Esquivels' *casa grande* for several days of watching *vaqueros* display their talents with horses and cattle. Esteban Esquivel's horsemanship was famous throughout the region.

Lieutenant Ochoa dismounted, spoke to the *alcalde* a moment or two, greeted Father Martín, then set up a table under the church portico and opened a large ledger. We were roused from our rest and marched to the dainty commander. Each man was examined for general health and the condition of his teeth, then was either excused or pressed into service, sealing the deal by making his mark in the ledger. Esteban Esquivel stood beside the lieutenant, informing him whether or not each man was telling the truth. Though all of us worked for the Esquivels in one fashion or another, it was obvious that Esteban did not know anything about the men upon whom his family's fortune depended.

Several men were dismissed—a cripple, two men over fifty, one widower with seven children, four men with rotted or missing front teeth, five young men who claimed to be under sixteen, and a man who was so pale and nervous, he vomited near the *alcalde*'s foot to prove that he was too sick to travel. Of course, some of them lied. But who was I to condemn them to a fate that I myself did not want? Each time the lieutenant questioned a man's age or health, there was always a bevy of women and relatives swearing he was unfit for the army. It was up to Esteban Esquivel to help decide each man's lot. With each dismissal, the lieutenant grew more enraged.

"This is the most pitiful village I have seen, Señor Alcalde," he said to the mayor, as he removed his tall, stiff *shako* and wiped his brow with a delicate monogrammed handkerchief. "It is a miracle that you are able to survive with such sickly, old men and so many widowers with ten children."

The *alcalde* shrugged. "True, we are a pitiful village."

"Well, I tell you, I will get my quota out of San Javier, whatever it takes." He pounded his gloved hand on the table for emphasis. "Señor Esquivel, from now on I will show no mercy. No more excuses!"

When it was my time to stand before Lieutenant Ochoa, my knees shook and sweat trickled down my back and temples. My mouth felt as if I had swallowed a boll of ripe cotton. Out of the corner of my eye I saw Aunt Florencia inching closer to listen. My sisters stood beside her quietly, which I know was difficult for Dulcinea, who normally chattered night and day like a mockingbird.

I gave the lieutenant my name and occupation. Like everyone else, it was farmer. When asked if there were any circumstances that would exempt me from serving in the Mexican army, I cleared my throat.

"I am fifteen," I said. I saw Aunt Florencia nod her approval and smile at me, as if to say, *That should do it.*

"Señor Esquivel, what is your opinion? Do you know this boy? Is he telling the truth?" the lieutenant asked, his quill poised over the ledger. "We need strong young men like him."

Esteban Esquivel, whom I had only seen from a distance during my life, put his hand on his finely chiseled chin and looked me over carefully.

"He is very tall; even taller than I, sir. And his shoulders are as broad as those of an ox. I believe I have seen him working in the cornfields, hoeing rows faster than any grown man. And I think I saw him swim across the river once. I can truly say that I have never seen a fifteen-year-old boy quite so huge. It is my opinion, *el teniente,* that this boy is lying. Surely he is not fifteen."

Never have I felt such a wave of hatred and anger at one human being as I felt toward Esteban Esquivel that day. To him I was no more than a pack animal. When the sergeant examined my teeth, truly, I wanted to kick out like an angry mule.

Aunt Florencia gasped. She rushed forward, her eyes blazing with anger. "No, no, young Señor Esquivel, you are wrong," she protested to Esteban. "Lorenzo is only fifteen. He is big for his age, just like his father and his grandfather. It runs in the Bonifacio family; your father knows that. Lorenzo's father saved your life once when you were five years old. You came foolishly close to a bull and Juan Bonifacio scooped you up onto his broad shoulders. He took a scar in the leg for it. Don't you remember how tall he was?"

Esteban shifted his weight uncomfortably and averted his eyes. "Sorry, *señora,* if I was only five years old, how could I recall such a thing? Besides, none of that matters here. It has nothing to do with the age of this boy."

"*Por favor,* Aunt Florencia," I whispered. "Do not cause a scene." Perhaps it was my humble plea, or perhaps it was the muskets cradled in the arms of dragoons on either side of the table, but my aunt stopped her arguing.

"You shall pay for this, young Esteban Esquivel. You shall pay dearly." After a withering glance at Esteban that clearly shook his nerves, Aunt Florencia steered my sisters away and hurried toward her *adobe* hut. I could imagine her quickly getting out her black candles and preparing to chant a curse.

"*¡Bueno!*" The lieutenant swung the ledger around and pointed to a blank line. "Place your mark here, Señor Bonifacio," he said to me. The sergeant loosened the ropes binding my wrists.

When I hesitated, the lieutenant furrowed his brow. "Don't look so sad, *muchacho.* It is a brave and honorable thing to serve your country. I joined the army when I was seventeen. Our beloved General Santa Anna joined at sixteen. He was a general long before the age of thirty. Now, place your mark here, *por favor.*" He dipped the feather quill into a bottle of black ink and handed it to me. I did not know how to write and had never held a quill. It felt strange in my fingers as I made a squiggle that looked like a landing eagle. After I finished, the lieutenant scribbled something under the mark with a great flourish.

The lieutenant blew on the ink a moment, then looked up. His small black eyes swept over the eight men he had conscripted, those unfortunate ones who had no excuses or no family to vouch for them. The conscripts included two prisoners from the jail, serving punishment for petty crimes; two lazy vagrants who had no occupations other than drinking *pulque* and loitering in the streets; two unmarried men; and two married men.

"Sergeant Ildefonso, are there any volunteers?"

"No, *el teniente*," the sergeant replied in a loud voice. "None except for brave young Señor Esquivel here."

The sergeant nodded toward Esteban, who bowed lightly in return for the compliment. I was not surprised that Esteban had joined the army. After all, he was the son of a wealthy man. Such as he buy their way into the army and are promoted quickly. It was one of the ways in which a young man could make a name for himself. Of course, a common peasant such as myself, whose Indian blood forever burnished his skin, could never hope to earn a rank higher than sergeant, no matter how talented, wise, or hardworking.

"*Muy bien,*" the lieutenant said. "We are done in the village of San Javier." He slammed the ledger shut, placed it inside a leather satchel, then glanced at the sun. "We will move out in one hour. Sergeant, make sure all

the men have supplies and extra clothes and sandals."
He paused. "And Señor Esquivel, since your father so
generously provided us with a wagon and two oxen, I
put you in charge of overseeing the gathering of provisions for our long trip. It will be your first official duty as
a soldier in the army."

The dragoons ate the food provided to them as if
they were bears waking from a long winter. Afterward,
despite loud protests from the *alcalde*, Esteban Esquivel
ordered villagers to fill the wagon with corn, meat, *pinole*,
cheese, and anything else that the village had. It would
not have been so unfortunate had the provisions been
paid for in gold or silver, but as payment the lieutenant
scribbled something on a piece of parchment paper with
an eagle at the top—the insignia of the government of
Mexico. As the *alcalde* walked across the plaza, the paper
in his hand, I heard him mumble, "This government
promise to pay us is not worth the paper it is written
upon. If a man did this, he would be called a thief and
hung from the scaffold. But when the government does
it, it is legal."

In a little while the wives, mothers, girlfriends, and
children of the new conscripts arrived with bundles of
clothing, food, and gourds filled with water. Most of
them, intending to come along with us, also carried their
own belongings. Some even brought along pigs and
chickens, their most prized possessions.

It is always such with the Mexican army when they

march to war. These *soldaderas* will follow their men wherever they go, no matter what the conditions, doing the cooking, washing, sewing, carrying heavy supplies, and tending the wounded. The generals know that married men with families make the worst soldiers because they look for any opportunity to desert and run back home. By allowing the women and children to travel with the army, the desertion rate is greatly reduced.

I saw Aunt Florencia and my sisters joining the noisy flock of women, their possessions wrapped in their *rebozos* and slung over their shoulders. Aunt Florencia was also toting a large basket filled with medicinal herbs and potions.

"What are you doing?" I called out.

"We are coming with you, Lorenzo," Aracelia shouted excitedly, with a heavy lisp, for her loose front teeth had recently fallen out. She was smiling as if it were a grand adventure. Dulcinea waved and grinned, too, her small legs hurrying to keep up with Aunt Florencia's long strides.

"No!" I shouted. "Aunt Florencia, stay here."

But my aunt stubbornly shook her head. "I am bringing along my medicines," she cried out. "The soldiers will pay me very well. I will probably make more money than a lieutenant's salary." With a burst of speed she rushed to the front of the throng, my sisters following close behind.

I swallowed hard, fighting back the wave of anguish

and guilt that washed over me. I had not wanted to drag my family into my troubles. Because of me, they were marching off to war. *War.* The word struck me like a bolt of lightning on a clear day.

"Where did the sergeant say we are going?" I asked Bernardo, one of the married men. He had been conscripted because he was a newlywed and did not yet have children. At first he didn't reply. He was furious that his lovely new bride had decided not to follow with the other women. I repeated my question.

"Texas," he snapped. "The sergeant said we are going to Texas."

"Where is Texas?" I asked, for I hardly knew the name of my own village, much less the names of distant states.

"It is somewhere north of the Río Bravo," Bernardo replied. "Someone said *norteamericano* settlers there are rebelling against Mexico."

This amazed me. I had never seen a *norteamericano*, and I could not imagine what a place called Texas had to do with my tiny village hundreds of leagues away.

THREE

Following
the Eagle

After the lieutenant called the dragoons to order, they mounted their horses and we moved out. First came the lieutenant with Esteban and two soldiers riding beside him, then the conscripts, then more armed dragoons, then the supply wagon, and lastly the women and children, carrying their loved ones' supplies on their shoulders.

Soon the dust from the horses' hooves stung my eyes and parched my throat. As we headed north, toward a group of hills, my little village grew smaller and smaller. By the end of the day, when the lieutenant ordered us to bivouac, we were in a valley and the village was no longer in sight.

The mounted soldiers unsaddled their horses, pitched small canvas tents, and made campfires not far from a small stream. The women, slowed by the small children and animals, had not yet arrived.

After our hands were untied, I dropped to my knees and stuck my face into the cool water. Realizing that this was the farthest I had ever been from San Javier, suddenly I felt alone. I was the youngest by far. The person closest to my own age was eighteen-year-old Esteban Esquivel, but that wealthy *criollo* was the last person on earth I wanted to befriend.

Before long the women arrived. We heard their chattering and the laughter of children and squeal of pigs as they came over the nearest hill. The conscripts walked out to greet them, and everyone found a spot to set up the cooking pots. I helped Aunt Florencia with her heavy basket of medicines. Her face was weary and her black clothes were covered with a thick layer of dust. My sisters wore only sandals on their feet, now covered with cactus needles and dirt. I scooped up their light bodies and carried them to the shade of a twisted oak tree.

Aunt Florencia spread out each girl's *rebozo* on the ground and the girls lay down, exhausted. Within minutes, they were asleep. I helped my aunt gather wood and start the fire. It was dark by the time she prepared a simple meal of beans, *tortillas,* and dried beef. Simple though it was, the food was delicious to a hungry boy who had not eaten for eight hours.

After eating, I took off my sandals so I could better rub my aching feet. The yucca fibers had rubbed the skin raw and tiny cactus needles had worked their way under the straps. I noticed Esteban Esquivel several paces away eating beef and sweet cakes that he carried in a leather satchel. I have no doubt that his meal was even finer than the lieutenant's. I saw him give his horse part of his cake as he stroked its white neck. No doubt Esteban was not used to such unpleasant conditions. His fine clothing, so fresh and clean earlier that day, was now covered in dust and sweat. For the first time, he looked like the rest of us. He looked very lonely. The villagers dared not speak to a person of such wealth, and yet none of the dragoons spoke to him, either. And the sergeant and lieutenant were too busy discussing plans to pay him any attention.

I was thankful that my aunt and sisters were here to keep me company. As far as I knew, Esteban did not know a single person in the camp. I almost felt sorry for him. Then I remembered that I would not be here were it not for his decision that I lied about my age. My sympathy for his loneliness melted like the Sierra Madres snows in summer.

After the late dinner, I saw the sergeant walking among the soldiers and new conscripts, speaking in low tones, much like a mother hen clucking to her brood. Across the camp a soldier played a soft tune on his *guitarra* and sang in a sweet tenor voice. Aunt Florencia nodded her head in rhythm to the melody. It was a popular tune that everyone in Mexico knew.

"Lorenzo, did you bring your flute?" my aunt asked.

"*Sí*. It is always with me," I said, patting a cloth bag around my neck.

"Play a tune for us before we sleep. Something peaceful."

I have played the simple bamboo flute since I was a child. My dear old grandfather taught me how. I am proud to say that I know more songs than anyone else in the village. Every time a stranger passes through, I ask what tunes he or she knows and memorize the notes. The music relaxes me in stressful times, and what can be more stressful than marching to war? I removed the flute from my cloth pouch and began playing a melancholy tune about doomed lovers. Aunt Florencia smiled and nodded her approval. It was one of her favorites.

As always when I played my flute, the sounds and sights around me vanished until I heard nothing but my music. I closed my eyes and poured my heart and soul into the tune until the final notes had drifted into the night sky, blending with the distant yelps of coyotes and the crackling campfires.

When I opened my eyes, I was startled to see that not only had Esteban Esquivel moved closer, but the stocky sergeant had stopped in front of me. In his hands he carried heavy ropes.

"*¡Muy bueno!*" the sergeant said, grinning. "Never have I heard that tune played so sweetly."

Esteban nodded. "Very nice, *muchacho*," he said in a soft voice. I was not sure that I liked being called a boy, but still these were the first words that an Esquivel had ever spoken to me, other than an order. I was too shocked to make a reply.

The sergeant motioned Esteban closer to my fire. The stocky man squatted down on his haunches, graceful in spite of his toadlike physique. I was amazed that his blue pants did not burst at the seams.

"You are the two youngest ones among us," he said, as the firelight flickered across his dark, round face, accentuating the thick black mustache. "You may think this is all a fun adventure, but I must warn you that young Lieutenant Ochoa is ruthless about deserters. This is his first war campaign and he takes his duties very seriously. There are sentinels posted all around the camp, and they will not hesitate to shoot you in the leg, or even worse."

The sergeant leaned closer, wagging his fat finger. I smelled onions on his breath.

"Me, I have seen too much war to care if a man or two leaves," he continued in a low voice. "Such a man does not make a good soldier and is a burden to the army, anyway. But the lieutenant will follow General Santa Anna's orders to the letter, no matter how irrational. Mark my words, any deserters will be punished without mercy, so don't even think of going back home to your *mamacitas* or your girlfriends." He smiled, revealing a gap from a missing tooth on the left side of his mouth.

"I have no intention of deserting," Esteban protested, a hurt expression on his handsome face. "I volunteered to join this campaign. I will soon work my way through the ranks and become an officer." His tone of voice was condescending and rude.

"*¡Bueno!* That is what I like to hear, Private Esquivel." The sergeant emphasized the word *private*. In a month or so, most likely Esteban would be an officer commanding the plump sergeant, but for now, he had to listen to orders. I could not hide my smile of satisfaction when Esteban's face clouded. I liked this sergeant very much.

Sergeant Ildefonso turned to me. "And what about you, *muchacho*? Are you going to desert? Do you have a little *señorita* waiting for you? Maybe that pretty goatherd, eh?"

I felt the heat creeping up my neck. "No! I have no girlfriend, especially her. And I will not desert, either. I am going to find my father." These last words surprised me as much as the sergeant.

"Your father is a soldier?" he asked.

"*Sí.* Conscripted nine years ago."

"I see. What battalion does he serve with?"

I sat up. This was the first time I had ever spoken to a soldier about Papa. "I do not know his battalion. No one has heard from Papa since the day he was taken."

The sergeant's mouth pursed a moment, then he shrugged. "We will see, *muchacho*." With a fond slap on my shoulder, the sergeant grunted and lifted his bulk upright. "You two will make fine soldiers." He glanced at my broad shoulders, the ones that had gotten me into so much trouble. "I think you will make a good sapper," he added. "A man who knows how to dig trenches and build earthworks is a valuable soldier. It is an honor to be in the Zapadores Battalion. I will talk to the lieutenant about it later."

I felt a certain fondness for this man and suddenly had the courage to ask a question. "*El sargento,* where are we going? Is there a war?"

"We are following the eagle. We go wherever she leads us."

"What do you mean?" Esteban asked.

The sergeant pointed toward the flag waving on a staff planted in the sand outside the lieutenant's tent. "The eagle on the Mexican flag. We are following her like the Aztecs of old. Don't you know the story about the eagle and the snake?"

Esteban shrugged. "I have no Aztec blood in my veins, why should I?"

The sergeant cocked his head to one side, then smiled. "Then I will tell you the story myself. Long before the Aztecs became the most powerful people in the Americas, they were homeless and wandered about for years looking for a place to settle. One day the Sun God,

Huitzilopochtli, told them to look for a lake with an island in the middle of it. And on a clump of cactus, an eagle would sit, a rattlesnake in its beak. That is where they were to settle and prosper."

"Did they find such a place?" Esteban asked.

"Of course. It became the capital of the Aztec Empire, and after the Spaniards destroyed Moctezuma's army, the town became Mexico City, our capital today. That same eagle is on the Mexican flag. And General Santa Anna also calls himself 'the Eagle,' for he admires the power of that beautiful bird."

"And where is the eagle leading us this time?" Esteban asked.

"To the city of San Luis Potosí, where Santa Anna has ordered all the battalions to muster. Then on to the province of Texas to subdue some unruly rebels. But it is better to keep your mouth shut around Lieutenant Ochoa and do not ask questions. He is strung tighter than catguts on a *guitarra*. Now, remember what I said about deserters."

The sergeant shook the strong ropes in his hands for a moment, then glanced over his shoulder. He lowered his voice to a whisper.

"My orders are to tie to a tree any man that I think may try to escape tonight. Obviously the two prisoners and the two vagrants are not trustworthy. What about you, *muchacho*. Can I trust you tonight?"

I nodded vigorously. The thought of ropes on my

feet and hands all night sent a chill through my body. The sergeant looked at Esteban, a question on his round face. "What do you think, Private Esquivel? Should I trust this one?"

I held my breath while Esteban looked me over. At last he nodded.

"I trust him," he said. "Besides, I am a light sleeper. If he tries to escape, I will catch him and bring him back."

The sergeant grinned. "Then he is your responsibility tonight. *Buenas noches, muchachos.* Sleep well. Reveille is at six o'clock." He tipped his hat toward Aunt Florencia, who had been listening quietly, my newly awakened sisters at her side and a black lacy fan covering her face. "*Buenas noches, señora.* May your dreams be as serene and beautiful as your face."

My aunt nodded but did not speak. I did not often think of her as beautiful, yet I suppose she was, considering that she was almost forty years old. Though the fresh blossom of youth had faded from her cheeks, she still had a fine figure and flashing dark eyes. I've heard people say that in her day her beauty stopped the hearts of men she passed on the streets of Guanajuato.

"I have never seen a *norteamericano*," I said to Esteban after the sergeant had walked to the next campfire to repeat his warning about deserters. "I wonder if they are good fighters?"

"It does not matter who we fight. Any war will do, as long as it helps me become an officer faster," Esteban said as he walked back to his bedroll. He rolled up his blanket to form a pillow, then wrapped a wool *manga* over his shoulders. Its colorful, finely crafted borders must have taken weeks for some woman to embroider.

It took me a moment to make up my mind, but at last I cleared my throat and said, "Thank you for vouching for me. I promise not to run away."

Esteban did not reply. Whether it was because he was asleep or because he did not care, I did not know.

Aunt Florencia and my sisters kissed me good night, then knelt to say their prayers. Their soft murmurs drifted on the wind and reminded me of home. Though I did not want them to be following me to war, I must confess their presence made me feel warm and secure. As I stared at the brilliant stars, I thought, *Maybe being in the army isn't so bad. We are hundreds of leagues away from Texas. Maybe the war will be over before we arrive.* Soon my eyelids were too heavy to keep open. But just before drifting to sleep, I heard voices nearby, speaking in low tones. I recognized one as the voice of Bernardo, the young bridegroom.

"I am not going to stay," Bernardo whispered. "They did not find my hidden knife. Tonight when the sergeant is asleep, I will cut my bonds and slip away into the desert. I will be back in María's arms by midnight tomorrow. I know that dog José plans to crawl into her bed while I am away. What a surprise I will have for him."

34

"No, Bernardo, you had better not try that," another voice pleaded. "The sergeant said the penalty for desertion is severe. What good will you do María if you are in prison or dead?"

"The lieutenant does not know me from a coyote. I was dragged from the fields like you and am no more than a stray dog to him. He will not miss me."

"You are a fool, Bernardo," the other man said. "If the sentinels do not catch you, then surely the Chichimeca Indians will And believe me, they will not give you the pleasure of a quick death."

"Perhaps death is better than ten years in the Mexican army." Bernardo's words were the last thing I heard before falling into a deep, hard sleep.

FOUR

The Deserters

Early the next morning, before I was quite awake, I smelled a musky, unpleasant odor. Then I heard the clank of a bell and felt something wet on my face. I opened my eyes and met the deep yellow gaze of a goat. I yelped. The goat let out a loud, "*Naaaaa!*" and stepped on my stomach as it ran away.

A familiar laugh cascaded around me. I rubbed my eyes and squinted in the pale predawn light.

"Catalina?" I stared at the plump girl seated on a tree stump, a rolled-up *tortilla* in one hand, a tin cup of steaming black coffee in the other. She smiled and rose to her feet.

"*Buenos días, mi amigo*," she said, and handed me the food and coffee. "How did you sleep?"

"I had nightmares about goats," I replied as I took the food. "What are you doing here?"

"I am a *soldadera*," she announced proudly, as if it were a great accomplishment.

"But why? You have no family in the army to follow." I sipped the coffee. It was too bitter. The *tortilla* was stale and the beans cold. A typical meal prepared by Catalina. Cooking was not one of her talents. "And what have you done with your old grandfather? Did you shove him down the well?"

"*Abuelito* is alive and healthy. He said he wanted to follow the army, and I had nothing else to do," she said, nodding toward the tree under which Aunt Florencia and my sisters had slept last night. I saw an old man with a shock of white hair, stooping over the blazing campfire, rubbing his hands together and chattering with my sisters. Aunt Florencia poked at the fire, her lips tight and a look of annoyance on her face.

"*¡Ah, caramba!*" I muttered under my breath. Ever since his wife had died five years ago, Catalina's grandfather, Señor Sandoval, had been after my aunt to marry him. They had lived in the same town, neighbors for many years. After the death of Aunt Florencia's groom, they fought in the Revolution side by side, following General Guerrero to the ends of Mexico and back, sharing the same meager rations, sleeping in the mud and jungles, carrying guns and ammunition on their backs. Though Señor Sandoval was twenty years older than my aunt, he was still strong as an ox. No doubt he was enjoying following the eagle one more time before he died.

"I see you brought along the goats," I said, chewing the tough *tortilla.*

"Of course. I could not leave my friends behind. And *Abuelito* brought his fighting roosters and two piglets, too."

I shook my head. "This is not a grand adventure, Catalina. This is a war campaign. Don't you know that soon lead will be flying and men will be dying?"

"*Abuelito* is not afraid of musket balls. And he is not afraid of dying."

"*Madre mía,* have mercy," I muttered under my breath, threw out the foul-tasting coffee, and rolled up my woven straw *petate.*

At precisely six o'clock, the bugle sounded reveille. Those who had not already been awakened by goats or crying babies grumbled and rose. Soon the smell of boiling coffee and cooking *tortillas* filled the air. The lieutenant appeared from his tent, freshly scrubbed, his clothes spotless and unwrinkled.

At seven, the bugles sounded the call to march. We strapped on our sandals and loaded knapsacks on our backs. A din arose of chattering women, crying babies, braying donkeys, grunting pigs, mooing oxen, bleating goats, squawking chickens, neighing horses, and barking dogs. The marketplace before a fiesta couldn't have been more noisy.

Sergeant Ildefonso moved among the mounted soldiers and conscripts on foot, pushing them into line and barking orders.

He nodded at me. "*Buenos días, muchacho,*" he said. "Where is your wealthy *criollo* friend?"

I glanced around but did not see Esteban. "I do not know, Sergeant. Besides, he is not my friend, and I do not want him to be, either."

The sergeant made a clucking noise with his tongue. "A man in war can never have too many friends. If young Esquivel offers his hand in friendship, better you take it. You will both need each other later on."

I doubted the sergeant's words but said nothing. I'm sure I was the last person in the camp that Esteban Esquivel would offer his friendship to.

About that time, a corporal ran up to the sergeant, his face shadowed with worry. "*El sargento,* two men deserted last night."

I immediately looked around and saw that Bernardo was missing. *¡Bueno!* I thought, but said nothing. The sergeant gave me a piercing look, as if I were somehow responsible for this bad news.

"I guess I should have tied your young *criollo* friend up after all," he said, then angrily mounted his horse and rode to the lieutenant's tent. I heard the young commandant yelling from across the field. I did not want to be in the sergeant's boots at that moment.

We moved out slowly, the officers at the front, the

women and children and livestock lagging behind. The morning air chilled my bones, but I knew that soon the sun would make me wish for the coolness. We marched across rugged terrain as the sun rose higher and beat upon our heads relentlessly. Someone said we were following a road, but if a wagon or cart had been this way in the past ten years, it was hard to tell. Not a wheel track could be seen in the sand.

My legs ached and sweat soaked my white cotton shirt and pants. Sand and pebbles slid into my sandals and more cactus needles lodged between my toes. My mouth felt like it was stuffed with cotton. I knew I should not drink from the gourd around my neck, for the worst of the day still lay ahead, but I could not help myself. At ten-thirty, when we stopped for *almuerzo,* or what some call a second breakfast, my water gourd was almost empty.

Luckily there was a creek nearby, though a pitifully small one. Here it was made apparent just how important we were in the eyes of Lieutenant Ochoa—he ordered the horses to drink first. Then the soldiers drank and splashed their faces and filled their canteens before we conscripts were allowed to take what was left. I cannot say that the taste of muddy water filled with horse slobber is refreshing, but I drank it anyway.

The women had fallen behind and were still out of sight. I collapsed to the ground. Using my knapsack to lean against, I ate cold *tortillas* and beans.

A few minutes into the rest, a commotion arose in

the road. I saw a rider on a dappled gray horse appear and recognized Esteban Esquivel. Behind him he was pulling a farmer in white clothing, ropes around his hands and neck.

"It's Bernardo," the man next to me whispered. "Poor unfortunate soul. I warned him not to desert."

The lieutenant rose, tugging at his blue jacket and replacing his *shako* on his pumpkin head. He waited under the only large tree in the area until Esteban rode up and dismounted.

"*El teniente*, I saw this man sneaking away early this morning," Esteban explained. "I followed him and found him hiding in a dry *arroyo*."

"*Muy bien*, Private Esquivel. I am glad to see that you are not a deserter after all. Indeed, you are an example of a fine, dedicated soldier," he said. Then he turned to the sergeant and scowled. "What happened, Sergeant Ildefonso? I ordered you to tie the unruly ones with ropes."

The sergeant's face flushed red and his Adam's apple bobbed as he swallowed hard. "I am sure he was tied securely. I do not know how he escaped, *el teniente*. I will be more careful from now on."

"Perhaps I should make Esquivel the sergeant and you the private, eh?" The lieutenant tapped the sergeant's barrel chest with his riding quirt.

The sergeant did not reply, but I saw his fingers tighten into a fist. "It will not happen again, sir."

Lieutenant Ochoa shouted at his orderly to bring a

whip, then placed it in Esteban's hands. "Since you found the deserter, I will give you the honors, Private Esquivel. Ten lashes. I will be lenient since it is his first offense."

While two soldiers tied Bernardo to the tree and pulled his shirt down to his waist, Esteban looked at the whip in his hands as if it were a writhing snake. Clumsily he uncoiled the long black leather, then hurled the whip at the prisoner. The lash landed lightly on Bernardo's bare back with a soft slap, like a woman's hand across the face of an insolent man. Bernardo did not even flinch.

Esteban wiped the sweat from his brow. "I'm sorry, *el teniente*," he said. "I am not experienced with the whip. Perhaps someone else..."

Lieutenant Ochoa stepped forward and examined the pink line across Bernardo's back. "Ah, I see Private Esquivel has much to learn about the secrets of the whip, but I cannot let this cur off so easily. *El sargento*, come. Sign your name on this man's back and show Private Esquivel how it is done."

The sergeant said nothing as he took the whip and stepped back, but his face was as gray as ashes. He gritted his teeth and his eyes flared with anger, whether the anger was for the lieutenant or for Esteban or for the deserter or self-hatred for his mistake of not guarding the conscripts well enough, I did not know. My heart pounded with fear for Bernardo.

With a deep intake of air and a grim face, the sergeant pulled the whip back and let it fly. It struck Bernardo's back with a pop as loud as a firecracker. The other soldiers shouted "*¡Ole!*" as if a bull had charged. Bernardo screamed in agony and a bloody red line appeared instantly on his back. The sergeant didn't pause but quickly raised the whip again. The pop, scream, and line of red made me wince. I felt sick.

After ten lashes, the sergeant stopped.

"Five more lashes," the lieutenant ordered. His eyes were wide with anticipation, and he rubbed his hands together.

The sergeant hesitated. "Five more? But, *el teniente,* the codes say—"

"I decide how to interpret the codes, *el sargento,*" the lieutenant screamed.

The sergeant clamped his jaw shut, then gritted his teeth as he obeyed orders. Bernardo jumped and screamed with pain each time the whip cut into his flesh. When the sergeant was finished, Bernardo slumped against the tree, his body quivering and covered with red lines and welts.

"Thank you, Sergeant Ildefonso," the lieutenant said, then turned to the rest of us. "Now, if any of you dogs want to desert, I vow that the next deserter will receive twenty lashes, and not from Private Esquivel. No, make that Corporal Esquivel, for a job well done." The lieutenant glanced at the deserter one more time, tugged at his jacket, then ordered the horses saddled.

While soldiers untied Bernardo and everyone prepared to move out, I watched Esteban. He was shaking violently, as if it were he who had received the whipping, not Bernardo. He walked to the creek, dropped to his knees, and retched. He dipped his hands into the water and splashed it over his pale face, then sat back and leaned against a log.

I wanted to stand in front of him and shout, "See what your meddling has done!" I had taken a step toward him, my fingers curled into fists, my eyes blazing with anger, when I felt a hand grab my arm.

"Leave him alone. He has learned his lesson," a soft voice said. I turned to see the round face of Sergeant Ildefonso. His dark eyes were focused on Esteban. Though I was but a lowly conscript, I could not hold my tongue.

"But he is so arrogant and selfish. He could have gotten Bernardo killed. And just because he wants to impress the lieutenant and rise up the ranks faster than a rabbit being chased by a coyote."

The sergeant put his hat on and swung onto his horse. "All you say is true, *muchacho*. But he is just a boy. I think Corporal Esquivel wishes he had a friend right now." He pulled the reins around and shouted the command to move out.

Esteban did not move. His face was still pale and he

held his hand over his eyes. I saw Esteban's gray horse grazing nearby. Feeling an unexpected wave of pity, I retrieved the horse and led it to Esteban. I stood in front of him and cleared my throat.

"Corporal Esquivel? We are moving out. Here is your horse."

Esteban lifted his head and blinked several times, as if he did not have the slightest idea who I was. As if caught asleep at his post, he quickly rose, dusted the grass from his britches, tugged at his jacket, and took the reins.

"*Muchas gracias,*" he said. He started to mount, then paused. "That man—the deserter...do you know him well?"

I shrugged. "Somewhat. Bernardo has the prettiest wife in the village. That is why he is eager to go back."

Esteban swallowed. "I did not know that the punishment would be so severe. I thought perhaps...perhaps being bound at night, or deprivation of food for a day..." His voice trailed off softly.

I shrugged again. "You must look at the good side. I am sure that Bernardo is grateful that you brought him back, for otherwise he may have been killed by Indians." I said this because I am cursed with the honesty of a nun, not because I wanted to ease his guilty conscience.

For a moment Esteban looked surprised, then a weak smile crept across his face. "You are right. Of course, I must look at the good side. Yes, far worse things could have happened. I feel much better now." He mounted his horse with a grand flourish.

His reasoning disgusted me. Another moment, and he would have convinced himself that poor Bernardo owed him thirty *pesos* for the privilege of being lashed. As I turned to walk away, he called out.

"Say, what is your name?"

The devil suddenly possessed me, and before I could stop myself, I blurted out, "What? You mean you do not recall the name Lorenzo Bonifacio? But according to you, you know me very well. You know my farming strengths, and you know my age."

Esteban knitted his brow a moment, then shrugged his shoulders. "Be assured, I know nothing about you, except that you play a flute nicely."

"Oh? You do not know the boy with the broad shoulders of an ox?"

A light suddenly ignited in Esteban's eyes. "Ah, yes...the boy who lied about his age. I will not forget your name again, Private."

Anger shot through me like an arrow. I opened my mouth to protest, but he spun his horse around, waving good-bye. He smiled and rode away, totally unaware that he had condemned an innocent boy to ten years in the army. I heaved a heavy sigh and grabbed my gear. It was useless to argue with a *criollo*. I was in the army and no amount of complaining would get me out. All I could do was vow to stay as far away as possible from Corporal Esquivel.

■ ■ ■

The column of men walked until about two o'clock in the afternoon, when the lieutenant ordered us to stop for *la comida,* the largest meal of the day. Afterward we would have a blessed *siesta.* We shed our knapsacks near a grove of shriveled oak trees at the edge of another pathetically small stream.

The sergeant passed out supplies and we started fires. Everyone was anxious for the women to arrive and cook the beans, soup, *tortillas,* and some meat. I chewed on day-old *tortillas* and drank coffee to stave off my hunger until the weary women and livestock caught up with us.

When Aunt Florencia finally arrived, she moaned as she lay down her basket of herbs and medicines. My sisters collapsed into my arms, their bodies damp with sweat and their clothes caked with dirt.

"Lorenzo, I am too tired to lift a finger," Dulcinea complained, as I carried her to my *sarape* spread under a scraggly tree. "We thought we would never catch up." Big tears rolled down her face, leaving tracks in the dirt.

"We ran into trouble," Aracelia lisped through her missing front teeth, as she slumped into my lap and lay her head on my chest.

"What happened?" I asked, watching Aunt Florencia

sit down and remove her sandals. Her ankles and toes were blistered and rubbed raw.

"Aayy—that crazy goatherd, Catalina. It is all her fault. A curse on her and that old man she calls a grandfather." Aunt Florencia made a sign in the air, then spat on the ground. "See, I am so dried up I do not have enough spit for a curse."

I scanned the arriving women, children, and livestock, searching for Catalina's plump face and her grandfather's skinny body. I saw neither. An uneasy feeling began to creep over me.

"Are they all right?" I asked.

"One of the goats ran away," Dulcinea explained. "Climbed up a steep cliff. Catalina went after it. After half an hour, she didn't come down, so Señor Sandoval went looking for her, leaving Aunt Florencia in charge of the goats."

"A curse on those goats!" my aunt muttered.

"After another half hour, the old man didn't come down, either," Dulcinea continued. "So I went after them. I found them. The goat had fallen into a deep sinkhole and couldn't get out. Catalina was trying to make the goat climb onto her *rebozo*, but it wasn't long enough. You never saw such a funny sight." Dulcinea burst into joyful laughter. Several people looked at her as if to say, *How can that child be so gay when the rest of us are so miserable?*

"How did they get out?"

"Catalina tied my *rebozo* to hers. We lowered her grandfather down into the hole. It took three tries, but he finally grabbed that crazy goat and we pulled them up."

"The delay cost us an hour," Aunt Florencia complained. "It's a miracle the Indians didn't get us. Señor Sandoval gave me his old pistol for protection." She patted her waist. Though she was exhausted, she began to cook a pot of beans, boil fresh coffee, and warm the *tortillas.* She shuffled on her sore, blistered feet. Her once-black dress was almost the same color as the dusty road.

"But where is Catalina now?" I asked, once more scanning the group of women, who by now had been joined by their men.

"As far as I know she and the old man are still looking for goats. By the time she returned, another young kid had gone astray, too." Aunt Florencia shook her head. "A curse on that old man."

When the food was ready, I told them about what had happened that morning—how Esteban had found Bernardo, the whipping, and how Esteban had not known my name. Aunt Florencia rose, wincing as she slid into her sandals.

"I must go to Bernardo," she said, quickly gathering her medicine basket. I took the heavy basket from her hands and carried it for her as all of us hurried to the place where Bernardo was lying. There was no one cooking for him. He lay on his stomach, breathing heavily, in too much pain to move.

"Bring water and food. *¡Pronto!*" Aunt Florencia ordered my sisters. She quickly began cleaning the deep red gashes and applying a soothing poultice of oil and mashed-up leaves. All the while she worked, she spoke softly to Bernardo. She washed his bloodstained shirt in the creek, then tore the cloth to make bandages. When she was finished, she made him sit up to eat.

After tending Bernardo, Aunt Florencia lit a candle and began mumbling prayers and laying sticks and special items from her basket on the ground.

"She's placing a curse on the lieutenant," Aracelia whispered into my ear.

"She will have to stand in line," I whispered back.

■ ■ ■

Later that afternoon, after a good rest, we started our march again. We did not stop until dusk. The women arrived not long afterward. As we always did, we ate our dinner late in the evening, around eight o'clock. While waiting for the food, men played cards and some sang songs. My sisters played games with sticks and stones. I noticed that Catalina and her grandfather still had not arrived.

The moon was full and high, casting an eerie silver glow across the silent camp. The soldiers had put away their guitars and most of the campfires were out. I was restless. I should have slept soundly, but every twig rustled by the wind, every whisper in the night, made me open my eyes.

It was well past midnight when I heard the clank of a bell. I shot to my feet and rushed to the road. I saw familiar dark figures coming toward the camp and sighed with relief. What did I care if Catalina and her stinky grandfather and her annoying goats had arrived? Quietly and quickly, I sneaked back to my bedroll. I closed my eyes and fell into a deep, peaceful sleep.

FIVE

A Thing of the Past

The bugle shattered my lovely dreams. I opened my eyes to see pale streaks of pink over the eastern *sierras*. Around all the cold campfires, men grumbled and moaned, while Sergeant Ildefonso chided and taunted them like spoiled children.

"Get up, you son of a mule, your mama isn't here to hold your hand today," he said, as his boot rousted one weary sleeper after another. "Time for beans, lovely beans!" he shouted, as he walked among the men, his broad flat behind and pudgy belly making him look precisely like a toad.

One by one the men rose, grumbling and complaining of the hour, the hardness of the ground, and the snoring of the men around them. I rubbed my burning eyes and stumbled through the motions of rolling up my straw mat and slinging my *sarape* around my shoulders.

We were higher in the mountains now and the night had grown cold, making my limbs feel stiff.

I looked around for the familiar goats and saw Catalina sitting on a rock, her face in her hands. It was very unlike her to be sitting still in one spot. Her old grandfather was pestering Aunt Florencia for a cup of coffee. I could hear their loud arguing.

As I walked closer to Catalina, I heard her soft sobs. I thought I should not bother her. I did not feel comfortable around crying girls. I started to leave, but she must have heard my footsteps.

"Lorenzo!" she called, her voice thick from crying. She pawed at her eyes and wiped away the tears. She stood. "Josefina is dead."

I opened my mouth slightly. I did not know who the unfortunate Josefina was, but now I understood why Catalina was crying.

"I am so sorry," I mumbled and removed my hat. "How did it happen?"

"A coyote killed her in the night."

"A coyote? Oh no." Josefina must have been a small child, for a coyote would never kill a grown human.

Catalina nodded, fighting back her tears. "Josefina was so sweet. You know, she was one of my favorites. I will miss her white beard and yellow eyes."

"What? You mean Josefina was a goat?"

"Of course. What did you think I meant?"

I shook my head and shoved my hat back on. "I should have known. Is she the goat that you rescued yesterday?"

Catalina nodded. "*Sí*. All that work and she died anyway. Do you not see the irony of it, Lorenzo?"

"The life of any goat is an irony," I muttered. "Perhaps next time you will leave the stray goat alone and not delay my aunt and sisters."

Catalina frowned and put her hands on her hips. "A goat is a thing of great value, Lorenzo Bonifacio. Someday when you have grown up, you will realize that." She turned and strode away, her goats bleating at me, as if to say they agreed with her.

■ ■ ■

We marched across rugged terrain all day as the sun beat down upon our heads. My legs felt like stones, and perspiration soaked my shirt. Most of the soldiers ran out of water. Even the most sturdy of the farmers, who were accustomed to hard work, felt their energy sapped from the grueling march.

That evening we met up with more soldiers encamped along a tiny stream. Several of their new conscripts were bound with chains, as if they were common criminals. Some conscripts were dark-skinned *indios* wearing the native clothing of their tribes. Their wives and children were traveling along as if they were going on a hunt.

Catalina offered to cook for us that evening. Aunt Florencia reluctantly agreed and stretched out on the ground beside my sisters. Though she did not complain, I knew that she was in pain. Her feet were bloody with blisters, so she had made the walk that day in her bare feet.

Catalina's cooking was terrible as usual, but she gave each of us a small piece of goat's cheese to break the monotony of the beans. I was so hungry, I gulped my meal in a few bites. While we ate, Catalina settled next to me. She nodded toward Esteban, who had selected an isolated spot, as if in self-exile.

"Why is no one speaking to Esteban Esquivel?" she asked.

"The men from the village do not know what to say to that wealthy, light-skinned *criollo*. The soldiers do not speak to him, either, because he was promoted so quickly. And the lieutenant hides away in his tent every evening and does not come out until daylight."

"Who is cooking for Esteban?"

I shrugged. "There is a cook for the soldiers. But I noticed that Esteban did not eat at *la comida*. Maybe he is sick."

"Poor Esteban. I am going to give him some food."

Before I could say "No!" and grab her arm, Catalina had risen and walked to where Esteban was slumped on the ground. I hurried after her.

"Señor Esteban, are you not going to eat?" Catalina asked softly.

Esteban opened his eyes and turned his head slightly to peer at us out of the corner of one eye. He shrugged his shoulders. "I am too tired to eat. Besides, beans and *tortillas* do not suit my taste."

Catalina held out a piece of goat cheese. "You are welcome to this cheese. Perhaps it tastes better than beans."

Esteban stared at the white cheese for a moment, then sat up and took it. "*Muchas gracias,*" he said with a nod of his head.

"*De nada*—it is nothing," Catalina replied. I thought she would be satisfied with her good deed, but to my horror she plopped down beside Esteban, as if she were his own sister. *Do only the daughters of goatherds have such nerve?*

"Everyone says we will pass through Dolores tomorrow, and there we will eat real food," she said in her chatty voice. I could not imagine that Esteban would be interested in anything she had to say, but he listened politely. "I am eager to see the town where Father Hidalgo started the Revolution. I have heard that the church where the *padre* gave his cry of liberty is an inspiration to behold."

Esteban snorted. "Sorry, *señorita,* but that is only a rumor." He swallowed the last piece of cheese and wiped his fingers daintily on his trousers. "We are nowhere near Dolores. But I must admit I am curious about Father Hidalgo. After all, my grandfather was murdered twenty-five years ago by that heretic priest and his brown savages in the town of Guanajuato."

I clamped my jaw to keep from cursing. Father Hidalgo is the most beloved of men to the poor Mexican farmers. His cry for equality for all Mexicans, both white and brown, and freedom from Spanish rule had started the revolution in 1810 that eventually brought Mexico its independence from Spain. Unfortunately, Father Hidalgo had been captured, tried as a heretic, and beheaded by the Spaniards. His head remained on display in a cage dangling on a hook in front of the granary for ten years in the town of Guanajuato, where my father and aunt had been born. It was the Spanish who killed Aunt Florencia's husband during their retaliation against Hidalgo's supporters.

Esteban glanced at me, smiling slightly.

"I see you do not agree with me, but that is to be expected. Your grandfather was not Spanish. Maybe he was even a follower of Hidalgo, eh?"

"Father Hidalgo was a hero!" I blurted out, unable to contain my anger. "Before his revolution we brown savages, as you call us, were no more than slaves to the white Spaniards. Maybe your grandfather deserved to die." I rose and took a fighting stance. Esteban shot to his feet, his haughty face now red.

Catalina leaped between us. "Please, Señor Esteban. Poor Lorenzo's uncle was murdered by the Spaniards.

You must be more sensitive." Then she turned to me. "And you, Lorenzo, know that Señor Esteban's grand-father was killed by Hidalgo's army. Put yourself in his place."

I felt fury building up in my chest. I knew that if I stayed another moment, I would explode. As I turned to walk away, I heard a soft chuckle.

"*¡Eh!* My brown *amigo,* do not be so thin-skinned," Esteban said. "Hidalgo's death is a thing of the past— twenty-five years ago, before you or I were born. That history belongs to the dead, not to us. All Mexicans— light, dark, and in-between—are equal now, are we not?"

I spun around and glared into that handsome face. With his intelligent brown eyes, light skin, and wavy black hair, Esteban would never understand what it meant to be *mestizo,* part Spanish and part Indian, with brown skin and straight black hair. He would never un-derstand what it meant to have your ancestors' customs and food and religion scorned and forbidden, to be de-nied schools and good occupations and political offices reserved only for those with light skin. Arguing with him would be useless.

I shrugged. "Perhaps you are right. It was in the past. Good night, Corporal."

I grabbed Catalina's hand and dragged her after me. I held tight until we were back at our campsite.

"Catalina, from now on, I think it best that we avoid the haughty *criollo* whenever possible."

She cocked her head to one side. "Are you jealous, Lorenzo?"

"Jealous? What a foolish idea. Only the daughter of a goatherd would say such a thing."

I returned to my sleeping spot and pulled my *sarape* up to my chin. The earth, still warm from the heat of the day, reminded me of my dear mama's oven. I closed my eyes and imagined her round body stooped over the hearth, her lips merrily chatting as she stirred a steaming pot of *caldo* or cooked fresh *tortillas* on the *comal*. Mama had died an early death because of Papa being taken away and because of the wealthy Esquivels demanding hard labor from all of us. Of course, I was not jealous. But how could Catalina even begin to feel pity for that haughty Esteban?

SIX

El Presidio

On the fourth day, another group of conscripted farmers was added to our forces. The new conscripts now numbered about one hundred—all from Guanajuato state. To an outsider we looked more like a gang of prisoners being hustled to jail than a group of drafted soldiers marching to battle. We conscripts had no uniforms. We had no weapons, no army supplies. We wore the clothing of simple *peónes,* and the closest thing to a weapon anyone carried was Catalina's cedar staff, which quickly knocked any man off his feet who dared to look at her wrong or to look at one of her goats.

On the fifth day of our journey, I awakened with a sense of anticipation. The night before we had seen the distant twinkling lights of San Luis Potosí. On the side of the nearby mountains, lanterns from the silver mines twinkled and faded like ghost lights. Each step we marched closer to San Luis filled me with both fear and excitement. Like the other conscripts around me, I had never been outside my own village, much less to a large city. I was tormented by a thousand possibilities, not the least of which was to escape into the crowded streets with my family and never be found again.

Also foremost in my mind was the idea that somehow I would be able to find my father among the throngs of soldiers. The notion had seized me on the second night and would not leave me alone. If it was true that most of the Mexican army was being assembled there, surely my father would be among them. I was determined to find him. And why not? Stranger things had happened—like seeing the Virgin of Guadalupe in the rings of a tree.

At last our column crested a hill. I looked down and gasped when I saw the city. Never in my life had I seen so many buildings. It was like something I had only heard about in tales, something I had never dreamed of seeing during my lifetime.

San Luis Potosí was a town of thousands of white, tan, and pale yellow square houses surrounded by mountains. The flat-roofed houses, some several stories high, were separated by narrow, winding streets and alleys. Occasionally a taller structure—a steepled church, a domed government building, or a fabulous mansion of some wealthy man—broke the flatness.

"*¡Dios mío!*" I cried out to the air.

Esteban, who was nearby at the time, began brushing

off his black hat and sleek trousers. "Well, I do not know about you," he said, "but I look forward to some good food—anything besides beans and *tortillas.*"

"I hear there are plazas with fountains and beautiful cathedrals," one conscript said excitedly. "I am eager to see such things."

The sergeant broke up our conversation and scolded me for dallying. A few minutes later, the bugler called us to order. We formed a straight column and began the march into town, two abreast. For the first time since I had been conscripted, I felt like a soldier. I squared my shoulders and fell into step with the other men.

At first no one paid us attention, except for a chili vendor and his children. The children cheered for the mounted soldiers in their blue-and-red uniforms, but pointed and laughed at us conscripts in our sandals and white peasant clothing.

When we reached the heart of the city, our troops turned down a cobblestone street. Gangs of barefoot vagabond children began skipping along in front of us, making noises like cannons and guns. Women leaned out of upper windows, some shouting compliments, some shouting unrepeatable obscenities. One woman threw a rose at Lieutenant Ochoa and it lodged in the mane of the black mare. He ignored it.

Another woman in a low-cut blouse leaned far out of a window, exposing opulent breasts.

"*Eh, soldados,* I have something for you, too, but it is

not roses." The woman laughed and made suggestive gestures. I felt my face turning red and wondered how much farther it was to our destination.

Soon the streets became narrow and twisting, forcing the men to form a single file. The buildings were so close together that occupants of the upper floors could lean out the balconies and hold hands with those across the alley.

"*¡Caramba!* Where are you all coming from?" a man shouted. "This is the fifth time today *soldados* have tromped down our street."

"What is going on?" another man cried out. "Is there another revolution? Who are we at war with this time?"

Lieutenant Ochoa ignored the shouts and changed the cadence to double time. Some laughing children reached out of the doors and windows, grabbing at the conscripts' sleeves and at the mounted soldiers' boots or the tails of the horses. The sergeant cursed them, and a few of the mounted soldiers kicked at small knuckles and hands.

Suddenly, I stubbed my toe on a loose cobblestone and fell forward, causing the men behind me to stumble and pile on top of one another. Laughter bellowed from the people in the windows. A woman carelessly tossed out her garbage without looking below, causing pieces of onion peel and corncobs to rain down. I heard the lieutenant cursing and shouting as the men struggled to untangle themselves and climb to their feet.

I tried to get up but stumbled again and landed on my knee. Sharp pain shot through my kneecap and brought water to my eyes. Behind me I heard Sergeant Ildefonso's familiar voice cursing everything in his path as he burrowed forward. He lifted me up in one quick swoop, then brushed a piece of corncob from my hair.

"Are you all right, *muchacho*?" he asked.

I nodded, too embarrassed to mention my throbbing knee.

The sergeant suddenly turned and shouted at the people in the houses, "You people should be ashamed. These are brave *soldados* who are going to fight for the glory of Mexico. They are your protectors."

"Heaven help us if they are our protectors," a man's voice cried out.

The sergeant swung around, looking for the man. "You should be cheering them, not throwing garbage. Why should they die for you when you act like this?" He glared at the people in the windows, who had grown quiet. Suddenly the sergeant bellowed at the top of his lungs, "*¡Viva México! ¡Viva la República!*"

First one person, then another, joined, until a chorus of voices shouted in unison, "*¡Viva México! ¡Viva la República!*"

The cheer sounded up and down the street and followed us until we stopped in front of a large stone *presidio* with heavy wooden gates, located at the opposite end of town near empty fields.

Beyond the fort, the pastures were filled with rows of canvas tents, soldiers in blue uniforms, and conscripts in white cotton. Cavalry horses grazed on the hillside. In a fallow cornfield, cavalrymen practiced maneuvers with lances that flashed in the sun. Cannons and howitzers had been placed in a field where artillerymen practiced loading and firing, sending smoke into the azure sky.

A tall, lean officer greeted Lieutenant Ochoa as we entered the *presidio*. The officer wore crisp white pants, a dark blue coatee with red sash and red breast. Elaborate gold trim and gold epaulettes on his shoulders signified that he was a colonel. On his head perched a bi-corn hat with gold filigree and a red-white-and-green pom-pom. At his side hung a saber in an ornate scabbard. His black leather boots glistened from a recent shining. Next to him the prim Lieutenant Ochoa, who had just dis-mounted his black mare, looked like a beggar.

After the colonel returned to the officers' quarters, the lieutenant ordered all of us conscripts to attention.

"Never have I felt such humiliation as at that display a little while ago," he said in fast, emphatic sentences. "You are untrained conscripts, it is true, but I will not have you acting like idiots who do not even know how to walk down a city street. From now on, you will act like soldiers." He jerked at the short front of his coatee as he paced before us like an angry jaguar.

I felt heat creeping up my neck and cheeks. Because of my clumsiness, all of the men were being chastised. I thought of stepping forward and confessing this fact to the angry lieutenant, but the churning in my stomach grew so strong I feared I would only vomit on his boots.

Lieutenant Ochoa paused, then drew in a deep breath and calmed his voice. "This is the *presidio* where the *Batallón Activo de San Luis* is currently garrisoned. Since you are conscripts, you will camp in the fields. You will be assigned to a company and regiment and receive equipment and uniforms later. We will train here for a few weeks and await further orders from His Excellency.

"You may think that because we are in a large city that you will be able to escape more easily. But do not believe it. You will remain with your regiment at all times. Because this is a campaign of war, any man leaving without my permission will be considered a deserter." He spun on his heels. "Sergeant Ildefonso, take over from here."

I felt deep disappointment at the lieutenant's words. I wanted very much to see the gardens and fountains and cathedrals. I followed the troops to the field, where Esteban and I were temporarily assigned to the same regiment; he to its cavalry, me to its infantry. Afterward, I claimed my spot of ground and spread my mat.

Not long after I had settled in, Sergeant Ildefonso walked over and squatted on his thick haunches. He put a hand on my shoulder.

"Why the long, sad face, *muchacho*? I thought you wanted to come to San Luis."

"*Sí, el sargento.* But how can a man see a city from here? If I dare to stick my nose out to smell a rose, the lieutenant will order my head blown off."

The sergeant laughed, the gap from his missing side tooth plainly visible. He looked at Esteban, who was shaking dust from his fancy cape.

"And how about you, Corporal? Do you want to see the city, too? Do you know that every night gypsy girls dance wildly and passionately?"

Esteban cracked a smile. "I would like to see the dancing girls, but . . . as the boy here says, it is impossible."

I felt a flash of anger. How dare he call me a boy. I had traveled the same distance as Esteban, had shared the same meager food and dirty water, suffered the same boiling sun. If anything, I was stronger than Esteban, who rode a horse and was not used to hard labor.

The sergeant rose with a grunt. "Ah, my bones are getting too old for this." He pointed to his horse, a big red gelding with a belly as round as his own. "Both of you see to my horse. His name is Valiente, and like his master, he has too much of an appetite. Do not let him eat all the food in the stable. Wash and groom him well. Check his shoes and clean his hooves. If you do a good job, maybe you will get a little reward." The sergeant rubbed his belly, as if the mention of food had reminded him that he was hungry. He hiked his pants farther up on his flat bottom and tugged his jacket.

Esteban led the sergeant's horse to the makeshift

corral and stable, where all the officers' horses were kept, then removed the saddle and bridle. He lifted each leg and examined the hooves for stones, removing a small one carefully with a pointed stick. He tossed hay in front of the red horse and began grooming it expertly. I felt a jab of envy. I had never ridden a horse, only a donkey, and once a mule.

"Valiente is a fine horse," I said, petting the soft red nose.

Esteban glanced at me from under the horse's belly, then snorted.

"My grandfather raised fine horses on his *hacienda*. Andalusians and Arabians. He was an excellent horseman and learned his skills in Spain. He taught my father to ride, and my father taught me. We have only two dozen horses now, but they are descended from the finest lines in Spain."

I wanted to say that "only two dozen horses" was unfathomable wealth to me. Three donkeys was a fortune to the average *mestizo*.

Esteban suddenly straightened. "I did not join the army to groom horses," he said with disgust. "If my family had not fallen on hard times, I would have studied at a military academy. I would have joined the army two years ago and would have been an officer by now. My grandfather would be so ashamed to see me doing this." He tossed the brush to me. "Why don't you finish this, since you admire this horse so much?" He started to leave, then turned. "And this is *not* a fine horse. This is an army horse, sturdy and practical."

In spite of the hard times, I could not imagine that Esteban's family was anything less than wealthy. I did not care what Esteban said; the big red horse was beautiful and very well mannered. I was happy to groom Valiente. I would have willingly traded all the goats in San Javier for him.

■ ■ ■

Later in the day, some of the new conscripts received orders to report to the nearest field for training. We followed directions as best we could, trying to learn the meaning of the many different drum commands, marching first in one direction, then another. At nearly every turn, we stumbled and fell over one another, much to the amusement of the regular soldiers, who watched from their tents in nearby fields, and much to the frustration of the sergeants barking orders. The sergeants insulted us, our sisters, and our mothers with every breath.

After an hour of drill, Sergeant Ildefonso called out a dozen regular soldiers in uniforms. Each carried a musket slung over his shoulder. As the drummer beat the different commands, the soldiers formed lines and marched in unison, skillfully turning on their heels, without missing a step, and flawlessly changing directions. They formed ranks, the first line dropping to their knees and the second line standing as they pretended to fire a volley. The next two lines stepped forward to fire, while the first two reloaded. They continued this display of firing and reloading until they had crossed the field. When they reached the far side, the drummer sounded retreat and they rushed back to the starting position. At the last drum command, they stood at ease, arms rested.

Sergeant Ildefonso singled out a young corporal to demonstrate the skill of loading a musket, aiming, and firing. His target was an orange-colored squash jammed on a pole at the far end of the field. The corporal swiftly loaded his long-barreled musket, aimed, and fired. The squash exploded into bits. The soldiers in the nearby tents cheered, while the conscripts watched in open-mouthed awe. The corporal then demonstrated the art of cleaning the musket and reloading. His hands moved faster than the eye could follow: tearing a paper cartridge open with his teeth, priming the firing pan, tamping the gunpowder with his ramrod. Once again he aimed and demolished a second squash.

After the regular soldiers were dismissed, the sergeant peered at the conscripts in our white cotton clothes and sandaled feet.

"Any questions about how to load a musket?" he asked, his hands on his wide hips.

For a moment no one spoke, then a voice from the back called out timidly, *"El sargento,* when will we get our uniforms and weapons?"

Lieutenant Ochoa, who had been watching the maneuvers from the sidelines, suddenly walked forward. He glared in the direction of the unfortunate man who had asked the question, then his dark eyes scanned the faces in front of him. When he spoke, he spat out the words like something foul tasting.

"You are the most pathetic group of miserable conscripts I have ever seen. You do not deserve to wear the uniform of Mexico. If I had my way, I would feed every one of you to the coyotes. And then I would draft the coyotes and put them in uniforms and give them guns. I wager they would do a better job than you *léperos*."

I felt my ears burning. *Léperos* was an unwarranted insult, as if being poor meant being disgusting and vulgar. I did not deserve to be insulted by a man with the head of a pumpkin. I wanted to shout at the top of my lungs, "Better not give us guns, *el teniente*, or we'll use your pumpkin head for target practice." The thought of it made me smile.

Suddenly I was aware of the silence around me. I looked up to find the lieutenant two feet away staring directly at me, as if awaiting an answer.

"I said, 'What is so funny that makes you smile?'" Lieutenant Ochoa demanded.

I swallowed hard and felt my knees go weak. "Nothing, *el teniente*. I was only imagining having a gun in my hand...shooting...shooting at an enemy. A *norteamericano*."

Lieutenant Ochoa did not smile. Instead he leaned

his pale face toward me. I clearly saw the hairs of his tiny black mustache and smelled the faint aroma of snuff.

"So, you think you are ready to handle a gun, eh? We'll see." He shouted at the nearest uniformed soldier, who was sitting on a rock, oiling his musket. The soldier trotted over and reluctantly handed his musket to me.

"Now, show me what you have learned, *soldado*," the lieutenant said, his hands on his hips. "See if you can hit the target."

As I took the musket, I saw the emblem of Mexico—the eagle and the snake—stamped on its lock plate. The gun was heavy, almost ten pounds. I squinted one eye and adjusted the long barrel until the remnants of the squash was in the sight. I cocked the flint hammer back and pulled the trigger. A loud click filled the air. Peals of laughter roared from the tents.

"God help us!" one of the professional soldiers shouted, and made the sign of the cross in exaggerated motions.

Lieutenant Ochoa growled and jerked the musket from me. "*¡El stupido!* What good is a gun without ammunition?" He quickly reached into the soldier's cartridge belt, removed a paper cartridge from the wood block, and shoved it into my hand. "Load the gun. Let's see if you were paying attention."

While I held the musket in my left hand, I looked at the cartridge with its premeasured gunpowder and a single lead ball in my right hand. My hands shook so violently the cartridge fell to the sand with a plop. More laughter burst forth. I felt hundreds of eyes staring at me and knew that every professional soldier prayed I would make a mistake, while every conscript prayed I would not. I pulled the hammer to half cock—that much I remembered. I tried to visualize the corporal a few moments ago loading his musket as fast as lightning. How I wished I had been paying better attention.

With a deep breath, I ripped open one end of the paper cartridge with my teeth, dropped the round lead ball down the barrel, then tapped in some black gunpowder, spilling part of it on the ground out of nervousness. I put the remaining powder in the firing pan and closed the frizzen, then wadded the empty cartridge paper and put it in the barrel. I detached the ramrod from the side of the musket and carefully tamped the powder and wad down as far as it would go. I replaced the ramrod in its slot, then turned to Lieutenant Ochoa. He had a smug expression on his face that made me even more nervous.

"Are you ready to fire?" the tidy man asked.

I glanced at Esteban, only to see his face pale and his eyes wide with terror. I scanned the other faces in the front row, but could not read their eyes.

"*Sí, el teniente,*" I replied. I turned back toward the target. Someone had placed a new round squash on the pole. It was larger than the last one, and for this I was thankful. As I drew the hammer to full cock and aimed, the uniformed soldiers nearby quickly stepped back, as did the sergeant and lieutenant.

"¡*Fuego!*" Lieutenant Ochoa yelled.

My heart pounded. I whispered an *avemaría* as I squeezed the trigger and heard the flint strike the plate. At once I saw a flash leap up from the firing pan, a pause, a hiss, an explosion, then a long fiery flame spat from the barrel, sending the burning wadding to the ground a few feet away. The roar echoed in my ears and at the same time I felt a kick and tasted gunpowder. For a moment my chest swelled with pride, then I saw that the squash was still on the pole. It had not exploded, nor fallen. It had not moved at all.

Lieutenant Ochoa stomped toward me, the look of an angry dog on his face. He jerked the gun from my hands, keeping it in an upright position.

"So, you think that's how you load a musket, eh?"

I nodded. "*Sí, el teniente.* But I missed the target."

Laughter rippled through the nearest tents. A feeling of dread swept over me as I watched Lieutenant Ochoa slowly lower the gun. I heard a lead ball rumbling down the barrel. The round lead dropped out of the end of the barrel and plopped onto the sand. The soldiers in the tents broke into riotous laughter and renewed their heckling.

"God help us!" the same soldier shouted again, and once more made the sign of the cross in the air.

Immediately I realized what I had done wrong. Waves of heat undulated over my face and neck. The air was suddenly thick and hard to breathe. I hung my head and waited for Lieutenant Ochoa to tell me to return to the ranks. It seemed like forever before the short man shot a glance at the tents and made a motion with his hand. The soldiers shut up.

"Return to your rank," he said, then turned to the others. "Let this be a lesson to all. You can be sure the *norteamericanos* will know how to load their weapons. They are expert marksmen. I've heard they carry a pistol on each hip, a musket over each shoulder, and a Bowie knife in their belts. And they can shoot the whiskers off a jackrabbit at fifty yards. That is who you will be going against. So I suggest you learn that the powder goes in first."

I slipped back into the ranks, wishing I could disappear. The sergeant demonstrated how to load a musket correctly, this time going very slowly and explaining each step. As we were dismissed, I felt every uniformed soldier's eye on me. One soldier performed a pantomime—aiming a musket and looking down the barrel for the ball. Another put a ball in the barrel of his musket and made it fall to the ground. His friends doubled over in laughter.

After dismissal, Sergeant Ildefonso made his way across the field. I wanted to run and hide. Maybe the sergeant was coming to chastise me and tell me what a fool I was. With dread filling my heart, I faced the stocky man.

The sergeant put his hands on his hips and cocked his head to one side. He studied my face a moment, then smiled.

"Don't look so sad, *muchacho*. Consider what happened today a good experience."

"A good experience? I do not think being laughed at by half the Mexican army is good."

"Ah, but it is. Tell me, which comes first, the musket ball or the gunpowder?"

I felt my cheeks burn. I did not know if this was a cruel joke, or if the sergeant was serious.

"The gunpowder," I muttered.

The sergeant smiled again and put his hand on my shoulder. "If this had not happened to you, you may have loaded your gun wrong in the heat of your first battle. And, more important, the other men will remember, also. They will think about Lorenzo Bonifacio being humiliated, and they will load their guns correctly. You are a hero. And you owe it all to Lieutenant Ochoa." He lifted his unruly eyebrows. "See. Now don't you agree it was a good experience?"

I thought about the sergeant's words, then shrugged.

"Maybe you are right, but I wish someone else could have been the hero."

■ ■ ■

Back at the camp, I crumpled onto the mat and buried my face in my *sarape*. I had not cried since the death of my mother three years ago. Crying was a childish thing, but at the moment never in my life had I wanted so much to let the tears fall. When I heard Esteban approach, I did not turn around. I did not feel like listening to the haughty *criollo*'s insults. I vowed if Esteban called me a boy again, I would plant my fist in that handsome face.

But when Esteban spoke, his voice was not full of disdain as I had expected. "You did much better than most would have," he said. "I was not paying attention to anything they showed us. If it had been me, the gun would not have even fired. Or it would have blown up in my face."

I sat up and turned around. I knew Esteban was lying. Rich families such as the Esquivels own many fine guns and know how to use them. I did not know what motives this *criollo* had for being suddenly kind, but for the moment I was grateful and accepted it.

"Have you seen your face?" Esteban said, pointing. I shook my head.

Esteban got up and retrieved a small square of tin

that had been hanging on a tree for the soldiers to use as a shaving mirror. He held it in front of my face. I saw the whites of two eyes glistening in a sea of black soot. I couldn't help but grin. My teeth looked like pearls. The sight was too much. Esteban started laughing, and I could not help but join him. I laughed until tears rolled down my cheeks. After all, it was all right to cry tears of joy.

SEVEN

El Presidente

Aunt Florencia and my sisters arrived that evening. They were forced to find a place on the outskirts of the campground with thousands of other *soldaderas.* Catalina arrived the next morning. Esteban nearly fell over with laughter at the sight of her chasing her goats down the streets, where they stopped often to nibble at flowers on porches and even to climb into windows.

As the days passed, the drudgery of camp life consumed my every moment. More regiments arrived daily from every corner of Mexico, until the hillsides were covered with dingy gray tents, blue-and-red uniforms, horses, cattle, mules, goats, pigs, chickens, and peasants dressed in white cotton. The battalions came from every region of Mexico, from the humid *tierra caliente* in the south to the rugged desert of the north, from the large cities to the simple villages. One battalion was made up of Mayan Indians from the tropical Yucatán peninsula. They wore seashells, bones, and animal teeth around their necks.

What a mixed group of uniforms everyone wore! No one regiment was dressed precisely like the next. Some wore new blue coats brightly dyed, others wore coats faded from years of washings and tattered at the cuffs. Some wore the new regulation uniforms, others wore obsolete uniforms from years past. Some uniforms fit too tightly, others too loosely. Every man used what he could find to hold up his pants and to cover his head. Even men within the same regiment did not wear the same clothing. It was impossible to look at a soldier and know exactly which regiment he belonged to.

On November 17, as I was chopping wood, I saw an entire division break camp and march to the town plaza, where they paraded to the lively beat of drums and fifes. The townspeople and other battalions cheered and waved their hats as the men marched onto the road leading north, their heads high and their eyes focused on the horizon.

"What does it mean, Sergeant?" I asked.

"It is the First Division under the command of General Ramírez y Sesma. He is marching to San Antonio de Béxar in Texas to join the forces of General Perfecto Cós. General Cós is in charge of the soldiers garrisoned in an old mission that has been converted into a fort. They call it *El Alamo*. The ungrateful Texan rebels assembled an army and have been poised outside Béxar since October. General Santa Anna fears the rebels will attack soon. You know, General Cós is El Presidente's own brother-in-law and it is a matter of family honor, as well as national interest."

■ ■ ■

By early December, every foot of ground outside San Luis was covered with tents, soldiers, conscripts, women, and children. No one knew the number of men for sure, but estimates were mostly five thousand, with another thousand already in Texas. Like most of the other conscripts, I still did not have a uniform or musket.

Whether I liked it or not, Esteban became my closest companion. Although Esteban was haughty, at least he did not mock me for being young. Some of the older soldiers insisted on treating me like an errand boy and expected me to do the most lowly of work. Because of our young ages, Sergeant Ildefonso treated Esteban and me like peas in the same pod and often gave us joint assignments.

Late one afternoon, Valiente threw a shoe, stumbled, and toppled Sergeant Ildefonso into a mud puddle. Cursing and grumbling, the sergeant put me and Esteban in charge of taking Valiente to the blacksmith for a new shoe, while he changed into clean clothes.

Happy to please, we dropped Valiente off at the blacksmith's shop and were told to return in an hour.

We walked behind the stables to a makeshift corral. I climbed to the top rail of the fence and gazed across the fields at the endless rows of canvas tents. It was growing late. The sun would soon set.

"Surely every soldier in the Mexican army is here by now," I said, then heaved a long, heavy sigh.

"What is wrong?" Esteban asked as he climbed up beside me.

"When we first arrived in San Luis, I dreamed of finding my father, but I have been looking for him for weeks with no luck."

"But how would you know him if you saw him? Weren't you just a child when he left?"

"Mama always said I have his shoulders and his chin. I have been asking every seasoned soldier I see." As if to prove this, I slid off the rail and approached an older soldier who was sitting on an overturned bucket, polishing his bayonet. Dust covered the cuffs of his blue pants, which he had raised and tied off with leather strips because they were too long. Tiny rips in his blue jacket had been patched with white thread in places and black thread in others. Two buttons were missing from the red breast front, and the pom-pom on his *shako* was ragged. The epaulettes signified that he was a corporal in the infantry.

"Excuse me, *el caporal*," I said. "I am looking for my father and wonder if you might know him."

The corporal did not pause as he rubbed the bayonet, nor did he look up.

"What is his battalion?" he asked. "Tres Villas? Toluca? Aldama? Matamoros? Guerrero?"

"I—I am not sure, sir."

"Then what is his regiment?"

I sighed. "I do not know, sir."

The corporal looked up, squinting one eye. "Are you sure he is in the Mexican army?"

"*Sí*, of course. His name is Juan Bonifacio, and he was conscripted nine years ago from our village in northern Guanajuato state."

The corporal returned to his work. "You need more information than his name. The army is full of men named Juan."

I felt heartsick, as I always did when I thought about my father and the hopelessness of ever locating him. I dragged my feet aimlessly toward a little hill behind the stables.

"You will find him," Esteban said casually, as he shook sand from his boot.

"But there are so many men. Sergeant Ildefonso says five thousand are here and another thousand are already in Texas. It is hopeless."

I surveyed the scene below. In every empty cornfield, regular soldiers in blue-and-red uniforms were finishing up the day's training. The sound of sergeants barking orders rose clearly into the air. Here and there men busily attended the artillery of each battalion—cannons of various sizes and howitzers. In the nearest field, a company of experienced lancers practiced their skills. Unlike other soldiers, they wore black hats with large brims and carried long pointed lances. They charged at make-believe enemies made of calabashes mounted on sticks. They shouted loud, blood-chilling cries as they pierced the round squashes.

Usually the sight of the lancers made my pulse race, but now my heart was heavy. I sat down and removed the flute from my shirt. I needed to hear some sweet, happy music to cheer my soul. I put the bamboo to my lips and began to play a lively tune. The tune had been my father's favorite and always reminded me of running through tall stalks of corn and playing hide-and-seek with Papa.

I did not think that anyone would be able to hear the music, but shortly the lancers glanced up and stopped their make-believe slaughter. They smiled and nodded in rhythm. One lancer used his musket as an imaginary woman and twirled around on clumsy feet. Then another company of soldiers noticed the music. Here and there, soldiers looked toward the hill, some paused and pointed.

I closed my eyes and played with all my heart, pretending that my father was among the soldiers. I imagined him running across the pastures, climbing the pile of rocks, and throwing his arms around me. I imagined him saying, "I have been trying to get back home for nine years. I have missed you more than words can ever say."

I felt tears building under my eyelids and quickly opened my eyes to shake them away. A soldier was coming toward the hill. From the epaulettes and the color of his collar, I knew he was an officer. My heart pounded. I stopped the music.

When the soldier reached the bottom of the rise, he put his hands on his hips and looked up.

"You, *muchachos.* Come down here!" he ordered in a loud, angry voice.

Esteban and I exchanged worried glances, then carefully climbed down. The officer, a captain, grabbed me by the shoulder.

"What do you think you are doing up there? This is not a *fandango*! Soldiers do not require dance music while they practice for war. Come with me."

This was not what I had expected. Now my knees began to shake as I followed the captain, who clung to my collar like a burr. Esteban trailed behind us, not quite sure what he was supposed to do.

We passed through throngs of soldiers to a large tent made of thick, shimmering brocaded silk. The emblem of Mexico—an eagle perched on a cactus, with a snake in its beak—was embroidered on the side of the tent. A beautiful white horse was tethered near the front, and the saddle on its back was made of fine leather and exquisite silver, elaborately carved and decorated. The horse shook its head and snorted as we approached. Its mane had been carefully combed and fell like silk around its muscular neck.

"Now, that is a fine horse," Esteban whispered to me.

"Wait here," the captain ordered, then approached the tent, where two sentries guarded the entrance. He spoke to someone inside the tent, then motioned for me and Esteban to come over.

As I lifted the flap and entered the tent, I smelled sweet cigar smoke and the tangy aroma of oranges. The furnishings of the tent were of the most exquisite na-ture—fine china, silverware, richly carved chairs, an ex-pensive oak table, even a silver chamber pot tucked in a corner.

Behind a desk sat a man about forty years old, taller than some, with a slender build, black piercing eyes, and a high forehead with receding black hair. His skin, like that of most of the high-ranking officers in the Mexican army, was the white skin of a *criollo*. He wore white pants and a long blue campaign coat with gold filigree embroi-dered at the cuffs and collar. His sash was a lighter blue with gold tassels. Diamond studs neatly lined his silk shirt. On the table nearby his bi-corn hat rested. Its up-turned sides were trimmed in gold. The white feathers and crest of red, green, and white plumes indicated that its wearer was a top-ranking general.

I swallowed hard. It had not occurred to me that playing a simple flute would cause such a disturbance.

"Your Excellency, here is the boy who was playing the flute."

The general put down a document he had been examining and looked directly at me, and then at Esteban.

"Which of you played the flute?" he asked.

I stiffened. "I did, sir," I said.

The captain kicked me in the foot.

"Always address the general as Your Excellency, or as El Presidente," he snapped.

My heart jumped at the words. Of course I had hoped to catch a glimpse of General Santa Anna, the most famous man in Mexico, from afar, but never in my wildest dreams had I imagined I would be in front of him being questioned about a flute.

General Santa Anna gave a disapproving glance at the captain, then ordered him out of the tent. He leaned forward in his chair made of dark mahogany and carved with eagles. He waved a finely shaped and groomed hand toward a silver bowl that was piled high with oranges.

"Would you care for a piece of fruit?" he asked.

Esteban and I glanced at each other. How long had it been since either of us had eaten a piece of fruit other than an occasional wild grape? The oranges smelled and looked so delicious that I felt my mouth watering. But perhaps this kindness was only a condemned man's last meal. I cleared my throat.

"No thank you, Your Excellency," I said weakly.

The general arched one eyebrow. "Really? I've never met a boy who didn't like a juicy orange." He leaned back in his chair. "I understand you are a talented flutist. Play something for me."

My fingers trembled as I reached into my shirt and withdrew the flute.

I tried to think of a song that would be appropriate for the president of Mexico, something grand and full of passion and honor, but my mind went blank. All I could think of was a simple peasant song about a boy who liked a girl named María. I put the flute to my dry lips. Though I had played this little tune a thousand times, I must admit, I played shakily at first; but as the music began to take over, I relaxed and played with feeling. The general closed his eyes and swayed his index finger in rhythm to the lively music that rose and fell like a flock of doves switching directions in the sky. When the song ended, the general opened his eyes and smiled.

"*¡Excelente!* You are indeed talented. What is your name?"

"Lorenzo Bonifacio."

"And who are you?" The general looked directly at Esteban, with piercing black eyes that could freeze any man's tongue.

"My name is Esteban Duran Esquivel. My father owns the *hacienda* lands where *he* lives," Esteban said, nodding toward me.

"Esquivel? Are you related to Don Beltran Esquivel of Guanajuato?"

Esteban nodded. "I am his grandson, El Presidente."

"*Bueno.* Why are you a mere corporal? A man with your talents should be an officer by now, no? Have you finished military academy?"

Esteban's face turned red. "I had to drop out of school. My family lost much of its fortune in the Revolution," he said softly.

The general smiled. "You have a lot to learn, Corporal Esquivel. You should have answered yes anyway. I would have found a sergeant's position for you this very day." He turned back to me. "You look very young," the general said, not with accusation, but calmly, as if stating a fact.

"I—I am fifteen," I said, lowering my head. I didn't think he would believe me, since no one else did. The general frowned.

"Do not be ashamed to admit your youth," he said. "I was sixteen when I joined the army, and a general before I was thirty. One brave youth is worth fifty cowardly men." He pondered his wisdom a moment, then quickly took a quill pen and scribbled some words on a piece of paper, signing it with a flourish. He handed it to me. I stared at the ink markings with wonder.

"Do you read?" El Presidente asked.

I shook my head. Only wealthy families like the Esquivels sent their sons to school.

"It is a special pass," the general explained. "Whenever I ask for you to come and play your flute, you will show it to whoever guards my quarters. Sometimes the trials and pressures of war harden a general's soul and make it difficult to sleep. I have always found music relaxing. Now, return to your regiment. If anyone questions you about your absence, show him the pass."

General Santa Anna reached for the fruit bowl and removed two oranges and handed one to each of us. This time we did not refuse. I knew exactly what I would do with mine. As we left, I saw a civilian man and a beautiful girl, about my age, waiting to enter His Excellency's tent. From the sad look in her eyes, I knew she did not want to be there.

■ ■ ■

Esteban and I ran to the blacksmith shop, but Valiente was not there. The sergeant must have sent someone to get him. It was dark; we had been gone much longer than an hour.

"We are in deep trouble now, my friend," Esteban whispered as we hurried to rejoin our regiment. "The sergeant will surely make us dig latrines for being so tardy."

We returned to our camp, but our regiment was gone. Apparently it had been moved again. This was not unusual. Every few days, as more troops arrived, regiments were forced to relocate.

"I hope we find our regiment soon," I whispered. "The smell of this orange is driving me insane."

"Why don't you eat it as we walk?" Esteban asked.

"I am going to give it to my sisters and my aunt."

"And the fair Catalina?" he said, laughing.

"Ha! After the last argument we had, I would not be surprised if she never speaks to me again."

After an hour of searching, we knew that it was hopeless. The campfires were low, and soon *toque de silencio* would be sounded. It was a dangerous thing for two soldiers to be wandering about after that final call. A few moments more and we were back at the stables. We had made a full circle without finding our regiment.

Esteban sat down and leaned back against a pile of hay. He removed the orange from his shirt and peeled it. The tangy aroma filled my nostrils with memories of Christmas, of Papa's strong arms lifting me up, of Mama cooking her special *pan dulce*, and of a joyful heart. It was now December. Soon Christmas festivities would begin with *la posada* in every town and village in Mexico. It was a terrible time to be going off to war.

"We will wake up before dawn and find the regiment before the sergeant knows we are missing," Esteban said, then pulled his cloak up to his neck and drew his hat low over his face. Soon his breathing was slow and even.

Unlike Esteban, I could not settle down. I tossed and

flopped like a fish on a riverbank, but at last I sank into sleep. I was awakened by someone rudely kicking my feet. As I opened my eyes I saw the angry face of a sentry who was pointing his bayonet at my chest. Another sentry did the same to Esteban.

"What are you doing here?" they demanded, a lantern held high.

"We are separated from our regiment," I explained. I stood, tugging my crumpled shirt. "Our sergeant sent us on an errand and we got lost."

One of the soldiers cocked his head to one side and picked up the orange peel. "Oranges? Only officers have oranges. Who did you steal this from?"

"The orange was a gift from His Excellency, General Santa Anna," Esteban explained. He folded his arms and glared at the soldiers.

The guards burst into laughter. "You need a better lie than that."

"I...I have a note...," I stammered as I reached into my shirt. The soldier jerked the paper from my hand, then stuffed it into his pocket without even glancing at it. It did not matter. I was sure he could not read it any more than I could. He turned me around, then stuck a bayonet at my back.

"March!" the guards commanded, and we obliged.

The point of the bayonet pricked my back like the tip of a yucca leaf. For several minutes we walked among sleeping, snoring men. At last we stopped in front of a stone building. It had four thick walls, with tiny windows cut high at the top. The front door was made of heavy oak, barricaded on the outside with a massive crossbar. Two heavily armed soldiers smoking cigarettes and playing a card game were guarding it.

When they saw us, the guards did not even bother to stop the card game. "What is the charge?" one of them asked between long puffs.

"Theft," replied the sentry who was sticking my back. He paused. "And throw in desertion, too," he added.

The guards, angry to have their card game interrupted, lifted the bar and suddenly I felt my body hurtling forward into a dark room. The smell of urine, sweat, bad breath, and liquor was so strong I wanted to vomit. I bumped into a man who cursed and threw a punch. Though the cell was pitch-dark, his fist landed firmly on my chest. I heard Esteban being thrown about, too, and the sound of fists landing on flesh.

"Esteban, where are you?" I whispered.

"Here," came a shaky reply. I followed the sound and found his shoulder. I pulled him to a corner. There was no place to lie down, so we slumped to the floor and sat. "Are you all right?" I asked.

"*Sí,*" he said, but I thought I heard pain in his voice. We said nothing for a very long time, then he chuckled softly.

"What is so funny?"

"All this because of your flute."

I reached inside my shirt and touched the flute. I wanted to tell Esteban that it was not the fault of the flute. It was the Bonifacio bad luck that had followed me all my life. It was the evil eye given to me when I was a child. But I knew he would only laugh more, so I said nothing.

EIGHT

The Importance of Goats

I spent a restless night full of frightening dreams and sudden awakenings, and choking on the stale air. Never in my life was I so glad to hear the roosters crowing and to see the gray light of dawn.

As pale light filtered through the tiny holes at the top of the one-room *calabozo*, I saw that I was surrounded by soldiers of every caliber, some in white cotton fatigues, others in uniforms. Most reeked of liquor, vomit, or urine. The stench made me queasy. I pressed my nose as close to the door as possible to catch a tiny stream of fresh air coming through a chink the size of a musket ball. Perhaps it was a musket ball hole. I did not have the sense to ponder such things at that moment.

"Are we going to be shot at dawn?" one of the uniformed soldiers asked in a trembling voice.

"If we are shot, so be it," said another soldier, a scrawny little man smoking a *cigarrillo* stub. "That is a better end than staying in this cursed army. We marched all the way from Tampico, and I have heard that our final destination is still two hundred leagues away. And over the most rugged mountains in all of Mexico. What kind of foolish general sends his men to war in the winter? Along the way there will be no grass for the horses or pack mules or oxen pulling the supply wagons. There is a rumor that we will go to half rations on the next march."

"It is all those women. Those *soldaderas* following us devour food like locusts," another man added. "They are like stones tied around our necks, slowing us down. They act as if it is a pleasant excursion rather than a war. They make men weak. They make us burn with desire to be in their arms instead of thinking about fighting *norteamericanos*. My wife is still in Guadalajara. I would never allow her to come on this march. And I would certainly never pay money to those *prostitutas* who are gathering for the long march."

I thought about Aunt Florencia and my little sisters and the other women from our village. They were good-hearted, hardworking women. They carried their loved ones' supplies on their backs and cooked every night. Without them, what a miserable lot we would all be. Even Catalina and her goats were a comfort, though I would never admit it to her.

I closed my eyes and envisioned Catalina's plump face and the ever-present bleating goats. I could almost hear the clank of the lead goat's bell.

I opened my eyes with a jolt. I was sure I heard a bell outside the jail. I pressed my eye to the tiny hole. I heard voices and saw women walking by on their way to the market at San Luis Potosí, balancing baskets on their heads. Catalina walked behind them, her goats following like obedient children.

Other prisoners heard the women, too, and rushed to the door, pounding it and calling out the names of their wives or lovers. "Catalina!" I shouted, but my pitiful cries were drowned out.

The noise had awakened Esteban from a deep sleep. In the dim light, I saw that his face was covered with bruises and his lip was swollen and split.

"What is it?" he asked.

"Women outside. I see Catalina and her goats, but she cannot hear me."

"Quick, play your flute. That instrument got us here; now maybe it will set us free."

I took a deep breath and played with all my might, hitting the highest, shrillest notes I could. I played Catalina's favorite tune, but she did not come to the door, and soon the women passed.

"Do you think she heard?" Esteban asked.

I shook my head as I put the flute away. "No. Or if she did, she is still angry from the argument we had."

"What kind of argument?"

"An argument about the importance of goats."

When the sun had risen, I heard the rasp of the

crossbar being lifted. The prisoners grew quiet and stepped back as the door swung open. The bright sunlight pierced my eyes like needles.

Sentries called out the names of five men and, at bayonet point, separated them out from the rest of us. The men struggled, but soon their hands were tied behind their backs and they were led away. Before the guard closed the door, I caught a glimpse of townspeople gathered twenty yards away. A priest was standing nearby.

"What is happening?" I whispered to the man smoking the *cigarrillo*.

"An execution," the man replied.

An officer's muffled voice came through the walls as he read a list of accusations. A moment passed, then came the loud commands of the officer, *"¡Firmes! ¡Listos! ¡Fuego!"*

A volley of gunshot pierced the air, followed by the gasp of the crowd.

I began to shake. "What was their crime?" I asked, trying to control the tremble in my voice.

"Murder. Desertion. Theft," one soldier replied.

"And which is punishable by death?" Esteban asked in a tight voice.

The man with the *cigarrillo* snorted. "In the Mexican army, everything is punishable by death, if His Excellency commands it."

A cold, sickening feeling squeezed my chest, making it hard to breathe. Soon the cell was filled with the sound of praying and sobbing. One man fell to his knees, clutching a crucifix.

"I cannot believe this is happening," I whispered. "If that guard would only show someone our special pass, we would be released."

"Guard," Esteban shouted through the crack in the door in his most proper, educated voice. "There has been a terrible misunderstanding, *señor.* We are not deserters. We had a special pass from El Presidente."

The prisoner with the *cigarrillo* laughed. "*Sí, sí.* I have a pass from His Excellency, too," he called out.

"And me, I have a special pass from the King of Spain," another shrieked.

The guard ignored the calls as he unlocked the door for the next party of prisoners to be herded to the plaza. The bodies of the first prisoners had been dragged away, but pools of blood were still soaking into the sand. With my right eye pressed against the crack, I watched the priest walking down the line of prisoners, speaking softly to each man. They mumbled prayers, except for one defiant man who spat on the ground and cursed Santa Anna. The firing squad leaned on their muskets unconcerned, awaiting the captain's orders. My knees trembled so much that I could hardly stand, yet some kind of gruesome curiosity kept me from turning away.

Suddenly a commotion erupted in the crowd. Some-one was pushing through the throng toward the jail. My heart leaped with joy when I saw that it was Sergeant Ildefonso, running on his stubby legs. He shouted for the guard to open the door and ordered me and Esteban to come out. I stumbled outside, squinting against the bright light and sucking in the fresh air.

"*Muchachos,* you are in deadly serious trouble," the sergeant said.

"We have a pass from His Excellency," I cried out. "That guard over there has it in his pocket." The ser-geant's eyes narrowed with disbelief, but he walked to the soldier nonetheless. In a moment he returned, hold-ing the slip of paper in his fat fingers.

The sergeant showed the note to the captain. A mo-ment later, the captain impatiently waved him away like an annoying fly and the sergeant bowed in gratitude. We did not have to be told twice to get out fast.

We trotted away from there like wild burros. As we reached the edge of the plaza, we heard the captain's sharp orders and the volley of musket fire, followed by groans and the sound of bodies falling to the ground. I started to turn, but the sergeant grabbed my arm.

"Don't look back," he said. "It is of no concern to us. They were murderers and deserters."

I wondered how many of the prisoners were inno-cent bystanders like me and Esteban. The thought of it made me shiver, but now was not the time to worry about the lack of justice in the Mexican army. I considered myself to be the most fortunate of boys. Perhaps the many years of evil-eye misfortune were coming to an end.

Not another word escaped from the sergeant's lips until we reached the bivouacs. Then he stopped and swung around. His face was red with anger. "That is the last time I put you in charge of shoeing my horse," he said, then turned and led us to the new camping area of the Guanajuato auxiliaries.

"How did you know we were in the jail?" Esteban asked at last.

"Lucky for you, Catalina heard Lorenzo's flute. She recognized the tune and came running to me. You owe your lives to her." He wagged a finger in our faces. "You should be punished for this, *muchachos*. You should have stayed with my horse until the shoe was on, then come straight back." He frowned a long time, then heaved a long sigh. "But now that you are close friends with El Presidente, I guess I must be careful what I tell you to do, eh?" He handed the note back to me, then walked away, shaking his head and mumbling.

I found Aunt Florencia's campsite. Catalina was standing over a pot of thick, black coffee while my aunt made *tortillas*. Old Señor Sandoval was teasing Aunt Florencia, telling her stories of the Revolution, trying to make her smile, a feat not often accomplished by any man.

Esteban did not join me. He said he had to wash the

stench of the jail off of his body. I walked into the camp slowly, my hat in my hand. I sat quietly on a tree stump. My sisters ran to me and threw their arms around my neck.

"Where were you all night, Lorenzo?" Dulcinea asked, as she pushed my hair back and removed a smudge of dirt from my cheek. "We were so worried."

"I was on army business," I said. I was too tired to tell the whole story. That would come later. I gave them the orange and their shrieks of joy made people all around turn and look. The girls quickly peeled the orange and split it with Aunt Florencia, Señor Sandoval, and Catalina. They offered me a slice, but the sight of the fruit only held bad memories now.

After my sisters returned to their chores, Catalina approached, carrying a metal bowl filled with beans, *tortillas,* and a small piece of meat. It looked like rabbit, but I thought it best not to ask what animal it might be.

"*Muchas gracias,*" I said, and devoured the food. When I had finished, Catalina took the empty bowl. She sat beside me, saying nothing for several minutes.

"How did you know I was outside the jail?" she finally asked, her eyes staring at the hillside where her goats lazily grazed.

"I heard the lead goat's bell."

She turned to face me and smiled. "Do you not have something to say to me, Lorenzo?" Her large brown eyes twinkled.

I had wondered how long it would take her to get to that question. "I am deeply indebted to you, Catalina. Thank you for saving my life."

She shrugged. "Oh, that was nothing. But don't you have something else to say?"

I let out a long breath. I knew she was leading up to this moment. I knew what she wanted to hear, and it was the one thing I did not want to say. If only I was not such an honest man. I stood up and released a long sigh of frustration.

"All right," I said angrily. "You were right. Goats are important."

"*Muchas gracias*," she said smugly, her pointy little nose in the air. "That is all I wanted to hear."

NINE

■ ■ ■ ■

A Rumor
of War

I was an exemplary soldier the next few days, trying to
make up to the sergeant for my foolishness. I cleaned
and shined his boots, brushed his hat, polished his
sword, and fed and groomed his horse. I carried buckets
of water to the mess wagon for the cook's cauldron of
stew and helped him peel onions and potatoes. I dug latrines and chopped wood. The work was humiliating,
especially to Esteban. He did not mention our night in
the jail. Only the bruises and cuts on his face reminded
us of that horror.

I noticed that Esteban had taken a liking to Señor
Sandoval and often came to visit the old man in his spare
moments. In spite of the fact that their families fought
on opposing sides, Esteban enjoyed hearing stories of the
Revolution and had a thousand questions about battles,
about courage, about dying. Especially dying. Esteban

had a morbid interest in stories about the last moments of dying men. I think in truth he was terrified of dying. Perhaps it is always so among those whose lives are easy and enjoyable. How strange that it is always they who start the wars and roust simple peasants out of their shacks to fight.

I had not heard any more news about General Ramírez y Sesma's division of men nor what was happening in Texas, though rumors abounded. The most disturbing rumor was that the government of the United States would send thousands of American soldiers to aid the Texans, though it was none of their business what happened on Mexican soil.

It was obvious that a major war was brewing, but if there was to be war, when would we receive our muskets, our uniforms, and, most important, our training? We new conscripts looked like a field of white cotton as we marched about, holding cornstalks instead of muskets as we learned the drum commands—one meant attack, one meant retreat, still another one meant no quarter.

The lack of weapons was a point that many of the men discussed at night as they sat around the fire, eating their meager rations.

"If we do not receive our muskets soon, how can we learn to shoot?" was the question most asked.

"If we do not have more military training, how are we supposed to know what to do in battle? Are we to fire at once? Half at a time, while the other half reloads? What is the procedure? What do we do if the commander is killed?"

"I hear we will be using British muskets so out of date that they are no longer made and the manufacturer is selling them at a bargain," one soldier complained.

"I hear that our uniforms are left over from Napoleón's defeated army— Heaven help us if we have the same fate as him."

The worries spread through our ranks like a disease, causing a general feeling of uneasiness and deep-seated fear. Eventually even the few training maneuvers became difficult because of the overcrowding. Most of the conscripts simply sat or lay about day after day with nothing to do except play cards and perform menial chores, while the uniformed soldiers practiced maneuvers.

"Why do we not receive the same training as the regular troops?" I asked a young corporal once. The man, thin and elegant in his uniform, merely shrugged. "Because the generals do not expect the conscripts to survive long enough to fight. All you have to do is fire one volley after another at the enemy. Your strength lies in your numbers. The more men the generals send forth, the higher their chances of winning a battle."

I thought about the corporal's words every night before I went to sleep. I could not believe the generals would sacrifice the conscripts so willingly, but as the days passed and we received less and less training, I knew in my heart that the corporal had been right.

I knew nothing of politics, but that is all that Señor Sandoval wanted to talk about. He explained to me that many citizens of the United States felt that Texas rightfully belonged to them because of the 1803 Louisiana Purchase, when France sold her holdings. Many thought Texas was included in the purchase, though it really belonged to Spain. It did not make sense to me that people were still arguing over something that happened over thirty years ago, but such is the nature of politics and war.

Often I was called to go to El Presidente's headquarters to play my flute. I was stricken with hopeless fear the first time, but by the third time I had been fetched, I was used to the luxury that surrounded El Presidente.

On these occasions, I never knew what mood would seize His Excellency. Sometimes he sat quietly, puffing on his opium pipe, his eyes half closed. Sometimes he had a pretty girl by his side and wanted her to hear the music, although he had a wife and family back on his *hacienda* in Jalapa. Other times he would be pacing, throwing his arms up, screaming at his orderlies. But the sweet flute music seemed to calm him.

Aside from the orange that had caused me so much trouble, El Presidente never paid me. The rumor that he was as cheap as a tin cup was true. He would rather have his fingernails pulled out than give a man a decent salary. Of course, when it came to his own luxuries, money was no object.

Every day His Excellency rode through the encampment to review the troops, to confer with officers and receive reports. He also enjoyed gambling at cockfights. He kept his own fighting roosters in large cages and treated them like prized pets. It was said that his roosters were better fed than the soldiers. At the cockpits, El Presidente mingled with the ordinary men, shouting and placing bets on his birds.

Señor Sandoval took his roosters to these same fights. One time he won ten *reales,* and bought all of us hot chocolate and fresh fruit from the market. But mostly he lost what little money he had. In the end he had to forfeit all his roosters and his pigs, and wound up with nothing to his name. He tried to borrow money from Aunt Florencia, who earned some funds from dispensing her herbal cures, but she wanted nothing to do with the old man. Señor Sandoval slipped out one night with one of Catalina's young goats and lost it in a gambling game. She gave him a thorough tongue-lashing and sold her gold earrings to get the little goat back. Sometimes I take great pity on Catalina for having such an unsavory grandfather. Other times I think she is very deserving of him.

Most of the soldiers played cards to relieve the boredom. They gambled away their meager salaries, or even their shoes and hats, when the money was gone. I am thankful I was never bitten by the desire to gamble.

On December 12, we were allowed to take part in the celebration of the Virgin of Guadalupe, the patron saint of Mexico. Peasants and native *indios* streamed down the hills in long processions, carrying the image of the Virgin in front of them. Indian men wore feathers and stone necklaces, while the women wore colorful embroidered skirts and blouses. They played flutes and shook gourds as they walked along. I attended mass for the first time since leaving my village.

Not long after the celebration, while I was playing my flute in El Presidente's tent, a brigadier general burst in. The officer had just received an important message from a courier from Texas who had ridden for days. El Presidente frowned at the interruption, but the urgency in his general's voice got his attention.

"Your Excellency, I bring serious news from Texas," the officer said, as he swept off his plumed bi-corn hat. "Your brother-in-law General Cós has waged a battle in San Antonio de Béxar. His men fought the Texan rebels in the streets and from house to house. The rebels drove our forces back to the old mission locals call the Alamo. His forces were surrounded by the Texan insurgents. General Cós's food, water, and ammunition ran out. He—" The general paused, his hands shaking as he handed El Presidente a written message. "I'm sorry to bring the news, Your Excellency, but General Cós has surrendered.

He and his men were spared, but he was ordered to leave Texas."

At this news Santa Anna rose to his feet so fast the girl in his lap slid to the floor with a silky swish. He brought his fist down on the table, rattling the lamp.

"*¡Caramba! ¡Qué diablos! ¡Idiotos!*" He spewed curses and stomped in front of the table, until the girl began to cry. "Get the devil out of here!" he shouted at her. She sobbed and ran from the tent in a flurry of ruffles and silk. Then he spun on his heels and grabbed the nearest object. With a scream he threw the oil lamp across the tent, where it smashed on the ground. A small fire burst up, and I quickly stomped it out. I did not need to be told to leave. I bowed respectfully and backed out of the open flap of the tent.

I hurried back to my regiment, not even bothering to show the sentry the signed pass. My routine of entertaining El Presidente was common knowledge now and went unchallenged. I gave the news to Sergeant Ildefonso and Esteban. A cloud passed over the sergeant's round face.

"*Muchachos*, this is bad news. His Excellency will not stand for such an insult to the people of Mexico. War is now inevitable. I predict we will leave for Texas before the end of the month."

Esteban and I exchanged wary glances.

"But it is wintertime. Surely El Presidente will not

march to Texas in winter," Esteban pointed out. "There is no grass for the horses or pack mules."

The sergeant looked at the sky, a crisp clear blue streaked with wispy clouds. "We must pray that the weather is always this good." He put his hat on his head. "We will suffer, *muchachos,* there is no denying it. But we must avenge our honor and our fallen comrades. We must fight for Mexico. Nothing will stop us now."

TEN

Feliz Navidad

A flurry of activity and excitement stirred through the camp. Men cleaned muskets and polished bayonets. They patched their clothing, repaired their sandals, shoes, and boots, and packed knapsacks. Blacksmiths shoed horses and saddlers repaired saddles for the cavalrymen; sutlers stocked supply wagons. Every man prepared his heart for war, and every woman prepared hers for tragedy.

General Santa Anna organized his army into two major divisions. The First Division, led by General Joaquín Ramírez y Sesma, had already left for Texas, in November. Obviously, his men had not arrived in time to rescue His Excellency's brother-in-law General Cós at San Antonio de Béxar.

The Second Division, the troops remaining in San Luis Potosí, contained three brigades, and each brigade was composed of battalions, auxiliaries, and miscellaneous elements. I soon learned that our regiment would be part of the First Brigade. The brigadier general placed in charge of us was General Antonio Gaona. I could not help but notice that many of the highest-ranking officers were foreigners—Italian, British, Spanish, Cuban. The general in charge of the entire Second Division, Vicente Filisola, was himself Italian.

My sisters were very disappointed that the traditional Christmas *posada* was being interrupted. But determined to have at least a small Christmas for the children, the women went ahead with their plans. On the night of December 16, a candle and lantern procession meandered throughout the camp led by a boy dressed as Joseph and a girl dressed as Mary, who was riding a donkey. Instead of going from house to house as was the usual tradition, they moved from tent to tent, singing *posada* songs asking for a place to stay. The group outside the tent would sing:

In the name of Heaven, I beg you for lodging,
because my beloved wife is too weary to walk.

The people inside the tent would reply:

This is not an inn, so keep on going.
I will not open this door, for you are just vagabonds.

The holy couple was turned away at each tent until they arrived at the last one, which was under a broad tree with tables set up for a feast. At the last tent, the people inside suddenly recognized Mary. They flung open the make-believe doors of the make-believe house and everyone sang and had a wonderful party and feast.

Normally, the *posada* procession would continue for eight more nights, until Christmas Eve, when the procession usually ended at the church for midnight mass. There a nativity scene would be reenacted with an infant placed in a manger surrounded by a cow, sheep, goat, pig, donkey, horse, and chickens. Boys would play the roles of the three wise men and the angels. After the midnight mass, all would celebrate with a feast, singing, dancing, breaking *piñatas*, and drinking. I did not know what plans Aunt Florencia and the other women had for Christmas Eve and Christmas Day, since we would most likely be on the move toward Texas.

■ ■ ■

Five days before Christmas, I noticed that Esteban was missing. Around noon he returned, not in his usual dingy pants and worn shirt but in the crisp blue-red-and-white uniform of the Mexican army. The dark blue wool still reeked of fresh dye. The pants and sleeves were too long and had been rolled up, but he was as dashing as ever a soldier could be under the circumstances.

"What is this?" I asked, and cocked my head to one side. "Are we being issued uniforms at last? Where do I go to get mine?" I could hardly contain my excitement.

An uneasy look crossed Esteban's face. "Some uniforms arrived this morning. But only enough for a few hundred soldiers. I'm afraid they have already been issued."

"Then how did you find out? How were you chosen?"

Esteban jutted his chin out. "El Presidente ordered that one be given to me. That is all I know. And he said that when we arrive at the next town, I will be promoted."

I felt jealousy and hatred rising and struggled to force the double-headed demon back down. After all, this was to be expected. I worked at a smile.

"Congratulations, Corporal Esquivel." I bowed ridiculously low.

The next day, I was overjoyed to finally receive my own musket. It was leftover British issue—an East India pattern—eighteen years out of date, but I cherished it as if it were made of silver and gold. I proudly carried it everywhere I went, even into the general's tent when I played my flute, causing His Excellency to crack a smile. That same day all the soldiers of the First Brigade received orders to dress in their uniforms, if they had them, and present their arms for inspection in front of General Santa Anna and his highest-ranking officers.

After the inspection I heard General Santa Anna recommend that each soldier should have an extra pair of shoes and a pair of sandals. Each man received a canvas knapsack containing dried beef, cornmeal, coffee, eating utensils, digging tools, an extra pair of cotton pants, and one extra pair of sandals. One blanket was tightly rolled and strapped to each man's back. The men also put whatever personal items they owned into the knapsacks—a crucifix, family mementos, rosaries. When full, the knapsacks weighed almost as much as we did.

As I packed my belongings into the knapsack, my heart beat faster. I had heard that the journey to Texas was a long one, perhaps two months, over very rugged terrain. I could not imagine how we would be of any use to the army in our current state, with no training. But the sergeant assured me that by the time we fought our first battle in Texas, I would be a good soldier.

But what if I was not a good soldier? What if I was a coward who trembled in his boots at the first sign of a battle? What if I dropped my musket and ran for the hills? These thoughts hounded me night and day.

■ ■ ■

The First Brigade was scheduled to leave on December 22, heading north for the town of Saltillo, the capital of the state called Coahuila y Texas. Two days later, the Second Brigade and sappers would leave, and on December 26, the Cavalry would leave. Because of this, the army would be spread out over a hundred leagues. Its front vanguard would be separated from its rear by days. El Presidente would ride with the vanguard, in an elaborate coach carrying his fine possessions, and many servants to wait on him.

As scheduled, early on December 22, sutlers' wagons filled with supplies and caissons loaded with munitions rolled into the plaza. The noise of chattering women, crying babies, bleating livestock, and shouting teamsters almost drowned out the drums tapping out the call to order.

Someone began a song, and we all joined in as our brigade reached the open road and turned north toward Saltillo. Ahead lay mountains, hills, ravines and valleys, and a long stretch of rugged terrain called *El Despoblado*, or the Uninhabitable Lands.

The sky slowly turned pale blue, streaked with pink and gold, revealing distant *sierras* shrouded in purple mist. The foothills were blanketed in a layer of golden brown grasses splashed occasionally with green shrubs, cactus, and a few trees, some dwarfed and twisted by the winds. An hour later, the singing had stopped, replaced by the clank of utensils, the slap of sandals, the creak of wagon wheels, the jingle of harnesses, and the crunch of hooves.

After four hours of marching without stop, Lieutenant Ochoa gave orders for us to break. As the orders filtered down the line of men, groans of relief filled the air. I stepped off the road to a clump of boulders, shaded by two crooked juniper trees. I removed my pack and collapsed to the ground.

"If I were a mule, they would shoot me," a soldier said nearby. It was a young man named Hector, from my village. Eating was his favorite pastime and he was as round as a pumpkin.

"If you were a mule, Hector, I would shoot you and eat you, I am so hungry," I said, as I leaned back against a boulder. A wave of relief flooded over my aching legs and shoulders. I rubbed my neck, which was raw from the knapsack's strap. I lifted the water pouch to my lips and sipped slowly. If I ran out of water, there would be no more until nightfall. I was tired and the urge to sleep was strong, but I knew I should eat or I would have no strength and the march would be that much more grueling.

I chewed my strip of dried beef and mixed some cornmeal with water to make a little paste. After eating, I lay against my knapsack, lowered my hat over my face, and closed my eyes. The sun was already hot, but there was a pleasant breeze.

The sound of boots crunching rocks woke me with a start. I looked up to see Sergeant Ildefonso's smiling face. In his hand he held a bundle of *tortillas*. He handed some to me.

"A gift from your beautiful aunt," he said, grinning.

"Surely the *soldaderas* have not caught up with us yet?"

"No. Florencia gave these to me early this morning before we left." He squatted on his thick haunches. "Tell me, Lorenzo, why is such a lovely creature as Florencia not married? *Dios mío,* a man would sell his soul for those eyes."

I shrugged and tried not to laugh. "Don't let Señor Sandoval hear you. He will be jealous and challenge you to a duel over the fair maiden's honor."

The sergeant made an obscene gesture. "That old man is half goat. Why would Florencia ever consider marrying him?"

"They have a long history together. I think he has loved her for twenty-five years. But do not worry, *el sargento.* Aunt Florencia will never marry again. She has told me this many times. She has devoted her life to medicines and helping the sick."

He nodded. "Yes, I have seen her helping the sick and injured along the way. She has done well with that deserter that I whipped. Does she blame me for that?"

"Bernardo's wounds have healed nicely. No, I do not think she blames you. You were following orders. My aunt can be very forgiving. Sometimes I think she would have been a nun if the nearest convent had not been so far away."

The sergeant sighed. "Such a waste." He rose with a grunt and started to leave, but I had one more question for the plump man.

"*El sargento?* Why are we marching so fast?" I asked.

"Because El Presidente plans to surprise the Texan rebels and end this war in one day. It seems to me he is

119

not taking the most direct route, but then my captain does not tell me everything. Who knows, maybe we will stumble onto the enemy one day." The sergeant replaced his hat and adjusted his pants. "We pull out in ten minutes."

After the sergeant left, I settled back and closed my eyes for five more minutes of precious rest. The memory of my father marching away from the village forced its way into my mind: the eyes damp with sadness, the prickle of his mustache, the smell of tobacco on his lips as he kissed me good-bye. I could not help but wonder why my mother had not chosen to travel along with him, taking her children. Maybe we would be with Papa at this moment had she done so. I would have to ask Aunt Florencia about this mystery the next chance I got.

The jarring bugle burst my daydream. I pulled on the knapsack and began the march again. How many more days would this pace last?

■ ■ ■

On Christmas Eve the general gave orders to pitch camp near a small river. I do not recall its name, but it was narrow and so full of stones and boulders that it was difficult to get to the water.

By the time the soldiers had pitched tents, dug latrines, and chopped firewood, the women had arrived. Although Dulcinea and Aracelia were exhausted, they hugged me and kissed my cheek. I guess I was the nearest thing to a father they had.

As it grew dark, after the meal and rest, the spirit of the camp changed. During the day the men were like marching cattle, brainless and without thought of anything except water and sleep. At night, when the women were there, it was a different world.

First there was laughter. And there was music. Here and there a girl would dance around a campfire to the clicking of *castañetas* and the rustling of petticoats as she twirled. Children darted about, laughing as they chased each other. Young soldiers strolled with girls. Older soldiers dined with their wives.

That night campfires lighted the fields like fireflies. I found Dulcinea wrestling with a little boy half her age. Aracelia was playing an old game. Two boys held their arms to form an arc while giggling girls ran under it. At certain times, the boys dropped their hands and captured whichever girl was passing under the bridge. The captured girl replaced one of the boys, and the song began again.

Señor Sandoval was once again at Aunt Florencia's feet. The goats had retired for the night under a low-hanging tree. I did not see Catalina, though I knew she had to be around.

Dulcinea waved at me. "Catalina is not here. She said she is too old to play *Doña Blanca*."

"Who said I was looking for Catalina?"

Dulcinea just giggled. "She is at the river with some soldier she met today. He's very handsome." She grinned, then winked at me. "But I don't think he's as handsome as you, Lorenzo."

I wandered to the edge of the river, where a white chalky bluff hung out over the water. I heard the soft music of a guitar and a young man's voice singing sweetly. I heard Catalina's laughter; I would know that sound anywhere. I felt a heavy thud in my chest and instantly grew angry at myself. Why should I care if Catalina was with a soldier? I had no feelings for her, other than annoyance.

I returned to camp just as Sergeant Ildefonso walked up to tell us bad news. The generals had ordered that there was to be no *posada* procession tonight. The men were to retire after *toque de silencio* so they could get an early start. My sisters could not hide their disappointment. I hugged them close and kissed the tops of their heads.

The sergeant knelt down and wiped tears from their eyes.

"Don't worry, *niñas*, we will have our Christmas Eve *posada* right now." He glanced at Aunt Florencia and winked. She nodded.

"You will be Mary," he said, draping a scarf over Aracelia's head. "And you will be Joseph." He put a walking stick in Dulcinea's hands. The girls giggled with glee as he lifted them up onto his horse and they settled in the big leather saddle. He handed me a lantern and I led the way. We sang all the *posada* songs as we walked from place to place, pretending everything was normal. Soldiers and other people along the way smiled and joined in. When we arrived back at our campsite, food had been spread on a blanket. And hanging from a twisted oak was a lopsided *piñata*. The small clay pot was decorated with wildflowers and weeds instead of colored paper.

Like little angels, my sisters did not complain but cheered and squealed with delight as they swung at the *piñata* and broke it apart. It had been filled with pecans and a few pieces of dried fruit. The sergeant had made it himself and spent his own money for the treats. To my amazement, Aunt Florencia laid out a *buñuelo*. Where she got the flour for the pastry, I still do not know.

There was no priest in the whole of General Santa Anna's army to give midnight mass, but Señor Sandoval said a prayer. My eyes began to tear. What a miserable, meager Christmas this was for my sisters, yet they pretended that all was well. I was suddenly overcome with love for these sweet *niñas* and quickly pulled them into my arms and hugged them with all my might. They did not question my strange behavior but kissed my cheeks and offered to share the pecans. We ate the food and laughed as if the world was right. When *toque de silencio* sounded, the good sergeant rose reluctantly.

"Muchas gracias, el sargento," Aunt Florencia said. He kissed her hand softly. She smiled—a miracle indeed.

After my sisters crawled into their beds, I lay awake, unable to sleep. The moon was beginning its descent when I heard a rustle of leaves near the river. I crept to the bluff and looked down to see a man picking his way over the boulders, glancing over his shoulder every few seconds. He slipped, raining pebbles to the river. He looked up. Moonlight reflected off his face and caught the blue of the sash around his waist. I had seen the blue sash many times. It had been woven by the fine hands of Bernardo's pretty wife, María.

Bernardo put his finger to his lips and his eyes pleaded. I nodded and whispered, "God be with you, *amigo.*" I made the sign of the cross and quietly returned to my bed. As I did, I noticed another man leaning against a tree looking out across the river. I prayed that he had not seen Bernardo.

ELEVEN

The General's Orders

We spent Christmas Day marching at an exhausting pace. With each day that passed, I expected to see Esteban riding up dragging Bernardo behind him. Many deserters were found and brought back, but there was no sight of the man with the blue sash.

On January 5, the eve of the Feast of Three Kings, my sisters placed their shoes beside their bedrolls. After they were asleep, Aunt Florencia and I slipped gifts into the empty shoes—cedar whistles I had carved, some nuts, and dried fruit. To my surprise, Catalina gave each girl a red hair ribbon. Early the next morning my sisters squealed with delight, though in my heart I knew they would have been happier with corn-husk dolls.

Catalina looked different that day. Her hair was freshly washed, combed, and braided into one long plait decorated with red flowers. Her red-yellow-and-blue skirt and white blouse had been washed. As the sunrise drenched her tawny skin in gold, I noticed for the first time that she was no longer plump.

"*Buenos días,* Catalina," I said softly. "The gifts you gave the girls are beautiful. Where did you get the red ribbon?"

For a moment her face flushed, then she shrugged. "My petticoat. But do not tell them."

I laughed, then with a surge of affection, I drew out a silk handkerchief that El Presidente had thrown away because of a wine stain. I had been saving it as a gift for Aunt Florencia.

"I know this is not much of a gift, but we have not been paid yet."

"For Epiphany? I am too old to receive a gift."

"It is a gift in appreciation for you saving my life. If you had not told the sergeant you heard my flute in the jailhouse, well..." My words trailed off.

As Catalina turned the handkerchief over in her brown fingers, the ends of her lips curled into a sweet smile. I know she saw the wine stain and the general's initials, but she pretended not to notice.

"*Muchas gracias,* Lorenzo," she said softly. "It is beautiful."

Catalina turned and peered at me with such intensity that my heart began to thump in my chest. How could this be? This was Catalina, the goatherd, whom I had teased all my life. What was wrong with my stupid heart? Suddenly I could not think of another word to say. I wanted to look away from her gaze and wished I were in a tree observing her from afar. But I noticed something in her eyes, something so sad that for a moment I forgot my own anxiety.

"Why are you so sad?" I asked.

She shrugged. "This day used to always be so special when I was a child. Now, it is just another day. I feel so old. I am already fifteen. I celebrated my *quinceañera* five months ago. Grandfather introduced me to the world, but no young men hurried to my doorstep. Most girls my age are already planning their marriages. Sometimes I think I will never find a good husband. Who wants a plain girl like me?" She lifted a baby goat to her lap.

I felt the blood rush to my face. "No, no. How could you say that? You are intelligent and... and—"

Catalina tilted her head back and chuckled. "I see you are having a hard time coming up with a reason why some man should marry me, eh? Well, it does not matter. As long as I have my goats. My grandmother used to say that a girl with goats will always find a husband." She stroked the tiny beard of the little baby goat as his head lay in her lap, his eyes closed in pleasure.

"You are worth more than the value of your goats. It is only a matter of time until some young man sees your true worth."

"Oh, there are many fine gentlemen who are interested," she said, her eyes twinkling. "The skinny corporal with the scar on his lip. The mango merchant I met in San Luis. He is fifty years old, but has a great need for a wife with goats so he can also sell cheese. Do you not think he would make an excellent husband?"

"Of course. If you like mangoes."

Catalina laughed a deep, wicked laugh that seized my heart. Just then the call to move out sounded. As I rose to leave, without warning, she stood on her toes and placed a quick kiss on my cheek, as soft as the touch of a butterfly.

My cheek still burned as I put on my knapsack. I saw Esteban leaning against a tree, smiling. He made a kissing gesture to the air.

"Mind your own business," I said, as we started the ruthless march again.

▰ ▰ ▰

That night, although she was tired, Aunt Florencia prepared rabbit stew, corn, and beans. She invited Señor Sandoval, Catalina, and Sergeant Ildefonso to join in the Epiphany feast. The sergeant had combed his hair back with some kind of grease and looked very dignified. He complimented Aunt Florencia so much that I was afraid she would chase him away, but to my surprise, she blushed and giggled. I could not recall the last time I had heard her giggle. Señor Sandoval was not very happy. I think he would have challenged the sergeant to a duel if Catalina had not kept an eye on him.

■ ■ ■

The next day, around noon, I saw a dozen black buzzards circling in a cloudless blue sky, their hideous red necks stretched toward a dark object beside the road. As the column of men grew closer, the stench of death crept into my nostrils. As we approached the motionless object, the odor grew stifling. I pinched my nose. Everyone walked faster.

When at last I saw the object close at hand, I gasped. A man lay on his back, his body bloated and grotesquely contorted. He wore the white cotton of a peasant, stained black with dried blood. The body was mutilated with arrows and the scalp was cut off, leaving a mass of caked blood. The buzzards had picked his eyes and his flesh, but I recognized the blue sash around his waist. It was Bernardo.

Poor Bernardo, now José will have María all to himself. I turned my head away and felt a wave of nausea sweep over me. I ran to the nearest bush and vomited, then blushed as I realized that no one else had done the same.

At the midday meal, the sergeant made his rounds, admonishing the men to watch for scorpions, to hide their food from coyotes and ants, to get a good rest. He did not warn them about deserting. He did not have to, for Bernardo's fate was on every man's mind. The sergeant stopped beside me, then squatted down and pushed his hat back from his face. Even the robust sergeant had lost weight. His pants hung looser, and he was using a rope to keep them up.

The sergeant looked at me a long time before speaking.

"You are not eating, *muchacho*?"

I shook my head. "I have no appetite."

"Because of the deserter we saw today?"

I shrugged. "Perhaps. Perhaps not."

The sergeant scooted closer. "Was it the first time you have seen a dead man this close?"

"No. I have attended funerals. My grandparents, my mother."

"*Sí*, but to die of old age or illness is natural, is it not? The sight of a strong man like Bernardo torn apart by savages and buzzards is something no young eyes should have to see. I know what you are feeling. I was the same way the first time I saw a dead soldier. I will never forget him—Amador Rodríguez. A soldier that I did not even like, but when his head was blown off by a cannon, I tell you, I vomited my insides out and could not eat for days."

"How did Bernardo end up here, on the wrong road home?"

"Oh, that is the way of the Chichimeca. They did that to taunt us."

I swallowed hard. "I liked Bernardo. He only wanted to return home to his pretty, new wife."

The sergeant gently placed a large, strong hand on my shoulder. Suddenly I could not bear my anguish another moment. I turned, my eyes glistening with water.

"I knew that Bernardo had deserted," I confessed. "I saw him that night at the river. I could have told you. You could have sent someone after Bernardo to bring him back. He might be alive now, if I had."

The sergeant pushed his hat higher on his forehead. "Sending soldiers after him would not have saved him. He had a small chance of getting past the Chichimeca, but if he had been brought back, he would now be dead for sure."

"What do you mean?"

"General Santa Anna issued new orders back on December 18. Because it is considered a time of war, the penalty for desertion is now death. Personally, I think it is cruel and unjust, considering how many poor soldiers were recruited from the fields at gunpoint. But a soldier obeys his general's orders."

A chill ran down my spine. "How can a general kill his own soldiers?"

The sergeant stared at the horizon a long time, then rose with a grunt. "You are very young, *muchacho*. After a few months, you will know all about El Presidente and his ideas about running an army. *Eh bien*, no point in dwelling on what cannot be changed, eh?"

The sergeant started to turn, but he paused, as if a decision weighed heavily on his shoulders. Finally, he drew in a breath. "I'll tell you something, Private Bonifacio, but you must swear not to tell anyone else."

I nodded. "I swear, Sergeant."

"You are not the only one who saw Bernardo escaping that night. I saw him myself. I could have gone after him. Like Bernardo himself, I was gambling that he would make it past the Chichimeca. It was a wager we both lost."

"Muchas gracias, el sargento," I muttered. How strange that I should be thanking the sergeant for telling me this. I am sure he thought that sharing the burden of guilt with him would ease my conscience, but it did not.

TWELVE

■ ■ ■ ■ ■ ■

La Llorona

The march continued, sometimes covering as much as fifteen leagues a day. Each morning I awakened to the sound of reveille. Groaning like the men around me, I would sit up on my straw mat and rub my burning eyes. In the dimness I would see dark forms rolling, sitting, and staggering to their feet and hear the curses and insults hurled at the bugler. Groggy from lack of sleep, I would shake out my blanket, wary of rattlesnakes, scorpions, or spiders, and would examine my knapsack, in case of thieves.

General Santa Anna and the vanguard of the army reached Saltillo on January 6. By the middle of January, the rest of the Second Division had arrived, too. Soon troops from other parts of Mexico joined them. Many were prisoners, for it was the policy of the army to empty the jails in every town they came to. No matter what the crime they had committed, from stealing a chicken to murder, they received the same punishment: service in the Mexican army.

On January 9, Sergeant Ildefonso stopped by the temporary corral where I was grooming officers' horses. The sergeant lowered his heavy body onto a bench and removed his sweat-stained hat. In his hand was a copy of the day's general orders and another piece of paper. As he read it, his eyes narrowed and his lips drooped into a frown.

"What is it, sir?" I asked.

"It is a circular from Mexico City. It says that *norte-americanos* in the United States are preparing to come to the aid of the rebels in Texas. They are holding meetings to recruit volunteers and are raising money for supplies and arms. Soon there will be thousands of them in Texas come to fight our army." He crumpled the paper.

"Are we at war with the United States of the North, then?" I asked, knowing that such a war would be long and far more costly than fighting a handful of rebels.

"No, we are putting down a rebellion in our own territory. It is no business of the United States what happens within our Mexican boundaries. It is like them to stick their long noses into our business, eh? They have the audacity to call themselves Americans, as if the rest of the nations in the Americas mean nothing. Well, we are Americans, too, aren't we?" He made a face and chuckled.

"Have you ever seen a *norteamericano*? Is it true they have long noses like armadillos?"

The sergeant burst into laughter and slapped his knee. "In fact, I did meet a *norteamericano* many years ago. He was passing through San Luis Potosí, a botanist gathering specimens of cactus and yucca and every plant he could get his hands on. Always scribbling in his little black journal. He spoke Spanish very well, but with a strange accent. He was taller than any man I have ever met, about six feet and with broad shoulders. His face was burned red by the sun, his hair was red, the color of my horse's hide, and his eyes were as blue as the sky."

I swallowed hard. "Six feet? Are you sure?"

The sergeant nodded. "I have heard that many *norteamericanos* are giants with big shoulders. Next to him I felt like an ant. But he was very gentle and eager to learn about our plants and how we use them for medicine. A very intelligent and interesting man." The sergeant stood and put his hat back on. "Do not worry about the tall *norteamericanos, muchacho.* All men are made equal by the guns in their hands."

■ ■ ■

For over a week, we camped at Saltillo and regained our strength. I saw the sergeant and Esteban less and less, for each day was filled with duties as the number of troops grew. Though the search for my father was always in the back of my mind, I had finally stopped asking older soldiers about Papa. It was pointless. Looking for one man in the Mexican army was like searching for a grain of rice in a basket of yellow corn. Yet I never completely gave up the hope that Papa was there somewhere in the crowd. I studied the face of every soldier who was the right age, though I did not even know for sure how old Papa was.

One night I asked Aunt Florencia why my mother had not traveled with Papa. Why we weren't with him now.

"Oh, she desperately wanted to," my aunt explained. "But she was too heavy with child, with Aracelia. In fact, she was so upset over your father leaving that she went into labor only two hours after he left. It was a difficult birth and your mama was bedridden for days. By the time your mama recovered, the army was too far away to catch up. Poor little Aracelia has never seen her papa."

My aunt's words brought back a long forgotten memory, something deeply buried in my soul—Mama screaming, uncontrollable weeping that lasted for days. My childish heart had thought her tears flowed because she was in pain from the childbirth. Suddenly I was filled with shame for ever having doubted my mother's love and devotion to Papa.

My time in Saltillo passed slowly, filled with boring routine during the days, card games, cockfights, and restless sleep during the night, broken by an occasional visit to General Santa Anna to play the flute. As the days passed, His Excellency grew more sullen and irritable. He asked his generals and majors for advice, then promptly ignored everything they said and argued vehemently to defend his decisions. Many a time I overheard loud arguing coming from El Presidente's headquarters and would see officers leaving with long, drawn faces.

One night, as I approached the camping place of my family, I heard Aunt Florencia chastising Dulcinea and Aracelia.

"What happened?" I asked Aracelia, who sat at her *metate* grinding corn.

"Dulcinea strayed down by the creek alone after dark. Aunt Florencia warned us not to do that."

"If you are not careful," my aunt said in a frightening whisper, "La Llorona, the Weeping Woman, will get you. She lives in creeks, rivers, and streams."

With wide eyes, the girls gathered around the campfire to listen to Aunt Florencia's latest tale.

"Why does she live in the rivers and streams?" Dulcinea asked.

"Because that is where her children died. She is looking for them so that her soul will be set free. A long time ago a beautiful young widow with two little children fell in love with a cold-hearted Spanish soldier. He told her he could never marry her because she had children. So in a fit of anger and despair, La Llorona threw her babies into the river and they drowned. She went to the soldier and told him, 'See, my children are gone. Now I can marry you.' But he pressed her, and she broke down and admitted that she had killed her children. In horror, the soldier told her he could never marry a murderess.

"La Llorona grew very depressed, for now she had nothing—neither children nor lover. She threw herself into the river, but when her spirit arrived at purgatory, the saints told her to return to earth and search for the children she drowned. So now every night she searches the rivers and creeks and streams of the land, looking for her children. She weeps and shrieks bitterly for them. It is said when you hear the cry of La Llorona, you will die within a month."

Dulcinea scooted closer to me, and Aracelia gripped my hand. As the girls trembled, I felt the hairs on my neck stand on end.

Aunt Florencia turned her attention to the *tortillas,* patting them out between her hands rapidly. "Now do you see why I do not want my little angels going to the creek after dark?"

"*Sí,* Aunt Florencia," the girls replied in unison. "We promise to never go to the creek alone again."

"*Bueno.* Now, if you want to fetch a bucket of water, ask your brother to accompany you."

The girls tugged at my hands and begged me to go to the creek. I picked up the bucket and led the way, while the girls held a lantern. It was a very quiet night, with a half-moon casting eerie shadows across the creek. Long clumps of moss hung from cypress trees, swaying lightly.

As I dipped the bucket into the clear, cold water, a sound pierced the air. The girls ran to my side, trembling and whimpering.

"It's La Llorona," they sobbed. "We will surely die soon."

I wanted to say it was just a silly legend invented by grandmothers and mothers to prevent their children from straying near dangerous waters, but part of me still believed the old tale.

"No, no. It is not La Llorona. It is only a panther crying for her mate. I have heard the cry of the panther many times. One lived in the mountains near our village, and every month she came down to kill goats. Catalina used to chase the panther away with a stick. Don't you remember that?"

"Are you sure?" Dulcinea pleaded.

"Yes, I am very sure. Now, let's get the water and go back before Aunt Florencia comes after *us* with a stick."

The girls giggled and picked up the bucket. When they returned to the camp, our aunt was waiting anxiously. She twisted her hands and her face was pale.

"Did you hear a scream?" she whispered.

"Aunt Florencia, don't worry. It was only a panther," Aracelia chirped as she and Dulcinea plopped the bucket near the fire.

Aunt Florencia forced a smile, but her dark eyes had

a look of fear that I had never seen in them before. We did not hear the panther again that night, and I thought it strange, for a panther makes many cries in the night.

▬ ▬ ▬

By the last week of January, all the troops from the far regions of Mexico had gathered at Saltillo except for those already in Texas. The generals reorganized the soldiers, assigning some regiments to new brigades, creating much confusion over where to go.

On January 24, General Andrade, who was in charge of the Cavalry Brigade, organized all five thousand troops into a grand parade. The citizens of Saltillo cheered and waved as we marched through the plaza. Girls threw flowers and blew kisses. I must admit, my heart swelled with pride. How different it was now from the day when I staggered down the narrow cobbled streets of San Luis Potosí two months ago. Then I was just another conscript, despised like a hungry coyote. Today I was a soldier marching off to war.

Two days later, the First Brigade resumed its journey, following the road to Monclova, the former capital city of the state of Coahuila y Texas. The Second and Cavalry Brigades left on January 28 and on January 30, respectively. The terrain grew bleaker and more inhospitable. Trees disappeared, mountains grew taller and more barren and rugged, forming high ridges. The road was good for wagons, with few stones to encumber the wheels and the oxen. But there was no pasture for the horses or livestock. The men did not talk among themselves, for they needed to conserve their breath for the grueling march.

The first day, we marched twelve hours and covered an unbelievable sixteen leagues, stopping at two *haciendas* and the village of Carretas. The march was more grueling than any we had made before. It was as if *el diablo* were chasing us, and if we stopped for a moment he would grab us and drag us down to hell.

For six days the grueling pace did not stop. The women began to fall farther behind, so I did not see much of my family anymore. At the end of each day I was too tired to do anything except eat a meager meal and sleep. I thought about Catalina as I drifted to sleep, but had she stood an arm's length before me, I do not think I would have been able to take a step in her direction.

Along the way, we passed an occasional *rancho* or *hacienda*. Instead of being welcomed with open arms, as I had expected, we were shunned. The First Division had taken the same route a month before, and the ruthlessness of General Ramírez y Sesma had left its mark on the hospitality of the people along his path. Sesma had taken cattle, pigs, goats, mules, donkeys, and horses without permission and without compensating the *rancheros* and humble farmers. He had taken corn and *masa* from houses, leaving the women with nothing to feed their children. There was little left for the Second Division, and even if there had been, the *rancheros* and farmers would have hidden it at the sight of the approaching army.

The sutlers' wagons were full of provisions, but no man had the money to buy the goods. Though food was furnished to the privates, it had to be shared with their families. The officers, whose salaries were higher, had to buy their own food and provisions, but it was priced unrealistically high. And since the officers had not received their pay in two months, some of them were as hungry as the common conscripts. Occasionally, out of pity, a few well-off officers bought food for their men with their own funds.

Lieutenant Ochoa complained, saying that a soldier should become hardened to the journey, but in reality we grew weaker with each passing day. We had already gone to half-rations. As the food supplies ran lower, we rationed more. Women dug yucca roots and ground them for flour. Men tried to kill rabbits, snakes, birds, rodents—anything to add to the dinner plate.

Many of the women carried equipment for their husbands. Some soldiers abandoned their knapsacks altogether, which were full of useless equipment anyway. Every day dozens of soldiers, women, and children fell to the side of the road in exhaustion.

Since water was so scarce, we had instructions not to give water to these miserable wretches on the wayside, for it was predetermined by El Presidente that they would die anyway. To him it was a way of weeding out the weak. My feet formed blisters upon blisters and ran red with blood. At least I had sandals. Most of the Indians were barefoot.

We marched forward, our aching legs moving without our heads knowing it. The sun parched our throats and cracked our lips. We thought of home, of girlfriends, of mothers, or sweet water and delicious food. Just staying awake was more than some men could do. I saw some who slept, their eyes closed, while their feet marched on.

If we ever chanced upon a pool or stream, the horses were allowed to drink first. Sometimes, after sinking our faces into the fetid water, many were stricken with horrid diarrhea, which only made them weaker. The most miserable of the lot were left behind to die. Desertions increased, but the thought of being left to the mercy of the roving Indians or being executed kept me from dwelling too long on the notion of escape.

The army's livestock, mostly confiscated from local ranchers, suffered unbearably. The cows stopped producing milk. The pigs ran off to find better food. The goats suffered, too, but not as much as the cattle and horses, for a goat will climb rocks to get grass and weeds from places where other livestock dare not go. And if goats are truly hungry, they will eat a man's clothing off his back.

The cavalry horses, however, suffered the most. Not as sturdy as mules or oxen, they grew thin and so weak that the cavalrymen fed them the straw from their sleeping pallets. The men walked beside their mounts carrying their saddles, for the beasts were too weak to support any sort of burden.

Esteban could not bear to see his beautiful horse suffering, so he left it at a farmhouse, saying he would rather another man have the fine Andalusian than see it die along the route. Esteban walked beside me now, his face drawn and haggard. He had not been promoted at Saltillo. Apparently El Presidente had forgotten his promise.

On the seventh day, as the eastern *sierras* turned pale pink with the morning light, I was awakened to a commotion rumbling through the encampment.

"What is happening?" I asked, as I sat up and stretched the kinks out of my back. The ground here, it seemed to me, was harder and rockier than any we had encountered yet.

"More deserters," a nearby soldier said flatly, as he quickly rolled up his blanket and slung it over his shoulder. "They creep out every night, like rats fleeing a sinking ship. These miserable wretches had the misfortune of being captured by the sentinels."

I felt a sharp lump rise in my throat and could hardly force myself to swallow a few sips of black coffee. This was not the first execution that I had seen along the way. Indeed, executions were a common occurrence now. But so far the executed conscripts had been strangers, men from other villages, from other companies, other regiments. The two men captured this day were men from my own village, men I had known all my life. I felt sick.

The bugle rang out and our regiment assembled, eyes heavy with sleep and fatigue. Mounted soldiers were leading the two men into camp like runaway calves, ropes around their necks, their hands tied behind their backs. I felt nothing but pity for the unkempt men with whisker stubble on their faces and dirt and blood on their white cotton clothes.

Lieutenant Ochoa walked to the men, his riding quirt in his hand. He paced a moment in front of the assembled conscripts, then turned.

"By the General Order of the Day for December 18, 1835, by His Excellency, President-General Antonio López de Santa Anna, I am instructed to treat all deserters as enemies of the state. In times of war, it is imperative that every soldier give his loyalty to his commander and obey orders without question. You are no longer an individual man, you are part of a unit that must function as one whole. If every part tried to think for itself and do as it pleased, soon the whole would fall apart."

His voice rose to a piercing crescendo, his face turned crimson, and he waved his hands for emphasis as he paced in front of the miserable-looking deserters. Finally he drew in a deep breath and jerked at his blue coatee. He touched his mustache then continued in a calmer voice.

"Accordingly, you are found guilty of the crime of desertion and hereby sentenced to death."

The assembled conscripts stood in silence, our heads hung low as a firing squad was called forward. Seven soldiers aimed their muskets at the unfortunate prisoners, who knelt, their heads bowed and their lips murmuring desperate prayers. Lieutenant Ochoa shouted the order, *"¡Fuego!"* and a sharp volley broke the stillness. The prisoners slumped to the ground. Red stains spread over their white cotton shirts and pooled on the sand.

A sick feeling rose in my stomach. I made the sign of the cross and fell into step as the column surged forward. I only glanced at the lifeless bodies, their blood still soaking the sand. I tried to feel something for them, but I could not. The dead men were no more real than the rocks on the roadside. I hated myself for feeling nothing, for not shedding a tear, but even my hatred was empty and cold.

THIRTEEN

White Death

By the time we reached Monclova on February 2, we had marched a total of fifty-seven leagues. Every man, woman, child, horse, mule, and ox was exhausted and scrawny. His Excellency, General Santa Anna, arrived three days later, accompanied by his personal entourage.

We were surrounded by *sierras* as bleak and gray as a mule's back. We were on the last leg of our journey. The next long march would carry us north, across the Río Grande del Norte, or what most call Río Bravo, into the land called Texas. If Texas looked anything like the rugged, mountainous region in front of us, I could not understand why anyone would go to war over its miserable soil.

In Monclova more prisoner conscripts joined the troops, these from the rugged regions in which we now traveled. They were a wretched-looking lot, in chains and ropes. It struck me once again how useless such men were as soldiers, for if a man was not willing to fight for the honor of his country, he was no better than a beast of burden.

When I asked Sergeant Ildefonso why prisoners were forced to serve in the army, he said, "El Presidente believes that in times of war, the quantity of soldiers is more important than their quality. He believes that whichever general has the most men will eventually win the battle. That is why he does not bother to train his soldiers. Any man holding a musket can shoot a volley, and it does not matter if he knows how to aim or not, if there are enough soldiers. They are merely fodder to feed the hungry cannons."

The sergeant's bitter words stung my heart. I did not care what El Presidente thought, I was not going to be cannon fodder. I was determined to learn how to use a musket skillfully and defend myself.

The weather cooperated and dropped to a cool temperature, refreshing our weary bodies. But we knew this respite would be short-lived, for the rumors said we would march again very soon.

A few days after our arrival, several soldiers, including Esteban Esquivel, came down with dysentery, a vile disease. The pounds fell off Esteban's already trim body, leaving him too weak to move. On the second night, Esteban lay on his back, shivering. No one seemed to care about his condition except Aunt Florencia. She was busy helping the sick women, children, and soldiers. Her supply of medicinal herbs was very low. She told me to take Esteban some foul-smelling liquid to drink. I gave the medicine to Esteban, then spread my *sarape* over his shaking body.

"*Gracias,*" he said weakly. "Stay here for a while, Lorenzo. I do not want to die alone, among these strangers."

"Eh, do not speak such a thing. You are not going to die. I have seen others worse than you who survived this cursed ailment. To tell the truth, I do not feel so good myself. Besides, if you are too sick to march, consider yourself fortunate. You will not have to fight in any battles." I tried to get a smile out of Esteban, but his pale lips did not move. He shook his head slowly.

"I dreamed of my death last night. I heard trumpets playing blood-chilling notes and heard the screams of dying men and the sound of cannons and musket shot all around. Then I heard angels call my name."

"Dreams mean nothing. If they did, I would be rich and married to the queen of Spain." I managed to get a little smile.

"I see what you mean. If dreams came true, I would have a beautiful girl in my arms, and it would be her lovely face hovering over me, not your ugly one."

I was glad to see that Esteban's spirits had been lifted, if even for a moment. Sometimes he wasn't such a bad fellow. He took his lack of promotion well. I think El Presidente had forgotten both of us altogether. I had not been called to play my flute in weeks. It was just as well. At that moment I could not bear the sight of the arrogant general.

Later that night I, too, succumbed to dysentery—a disgusting, foul sickness, which robs men not only of their health but of their dignity. Even the staunch sergeant had a mild case.

On February 8, when the First Brigade, along with General Santa Anna himself, left for the Río Bravo, Esteban and I, along with many more, were too weak to accompany them. The sergeant arranged for me and Esteban to wait until we were strong enough to travel. We were temporarily assigned to the Cavalry Brigade, which was staying longer because their horses needed rest. I was thankful that the sergeant was put in charge of the group of recuperating soldiers. I trusted him to look after us like a mother hen.

Aunt Florencia was delighted, too. Over the past weeks she had grown fond of the sergeant, and he was smitten with her cool, reserved beauty. Señor Sandoval had finally given up on winning Aunt Florencia over and had started wooing a young woman only twenty-five years old. It never ceased to amaze me that the old man was able to keep up with the grueling march. Though thin and given to sudden coughing fits, he matched the women step for step.

By February 13, I was well and had a ravenous appetite. My victory over death had humbled me, but at the same time had given me a new appreciation for life and an eagerness to get on with the journey ahead. For the moment, I felt invincible.

In spite of rumors of an approaching norther, the Cavalry Brigade, along with the remaining women and children, were ordered to march. The day began comfortably, but by late afternoon, the northern sky had turned a deep blue-black color and the temperature had plunged. The storm struck with fierce intensity, a howling witch wind with icy claws of sleet scratching at our faces. To make matters worse, the point men lost the trail and led the column in the wrong direction. The road, being narrow, allowed only one mule train at a time, slowing us greatly. By the time they had discovered the error and we had retraced our steps to the main trail, darkness had fallen.

By seven o'clock all was total blackness. I could hardly see my hands in front of my face. The soldiers wandered through a nearby woods in confusion, trying to find shelter. There was no leadership, for no one could see or hear the officers. The biting sleet had turned to snow, and the cold grew so agonizing that the foremost thought on every man's mind was shelter and survival. Some mule drivers took the opportunity presented by the confusion and deserted, leaving the poor mules in the freezing cold, their heavy packs still roped to their backs. Wagon drivers who stayed shirked their duties or left the wagons and oxen unattended.

Groups of soldiers huddled together on the side of a hill, trying to get warmth from one another. A few brave souls attempted to gather wood for fires, but the numbing cold froze their fingers, and the dampness of the wood kept it from burning well.

As I searched for sticks for firewood, keeping my hands hidden inside my *sarape*, I saw Catalina stumbling toward me through the swirling snow. Fog rose from her mouth, and her cheeks glistened bright red from the cold.

"Is Abuelito with you?" she asked, her teeth chattering.

"I have not seen your grandfather for the last hour," I replied. "Where are Aunt Florencia and my sisters?"

Catalina shook her head, and tears formed in her eyes. "I do not know. I came into the woods to gather some firewood and now I cannot find any of them. Please, you must help me look. My goats are lost, too."

Though my feet were icicles, I did not hesitate. I took Catalina's hand. It felt as cold as death. We stumbled through the woods, calling for my aunt, my sisters, and for her grandfather.

The deep, aching pain in my ears soon surpassed the pain in my fingers and toes. At least I had shoes on my feet; many of the men in the Tampico Regiment came from *la tierra caliente* and had never seen snow nor experienced anything colder than water from a stream.

After an hour of searching, we decided that her

grandfather and my sisters and aunt must be together, huddled around one of the tiny, sputtering fires. There were many people without fires, clinging to one another for warmth or crowded into hastily erected tents.

I saw Esteban in a circle gathered around a pitiful fire that provided little warmth or light. Catalina and I pushed in beside him. The snow, falling in great white sheets, soon smothered the blaze. To my left was a young *criollo* captain, who before now had kept himself aloof from the soldiers; to the captain's left was an Indian. They pressed together for warmth, for once forgetting the class into which they had been born.

When the fire went out, Catalina slipped between me and Esteban, and we arranged our *sarapes* over us like a tent. Sleep was impossible. Indeed, if a soldier did not shake off the snow every so often, he would soon be numb from the weight accumulated on top of his blanket. Some who fell asleep found themselves covered with such a deep layer of snow that they could not get out from under it without help.

When the long-awaited daylight finally broke, the air was clear and cold. The storm had passed, leaving before us a scene of the most indescribable and terrible beauty. As far as eyes could see, every hill and rock, every crevice, was blanketed in two feet of snow. Trees were completely covered, forming pyramids as pure as glistening white alabaster.

As the soldiers and civilians began to stir, shaking off

snow and standing up, the braying, mooing, and neighing of animals filled the air. Most of the soldiers had left their horses saddled. The animals were so covered by snow that they could not be distinguished one from the other.

Here and there the snow was stained red with the blood of helpless horses and pack mules. Many of the poor animals, exhausted and numb from the cold, had slipped on the icy ground, and when they tried to get up, the packs and saddles caused them to fall back, cracking their heads on the frozen ground. I saw Esteban beside a poor mule that had broken its leg. He spoke softly to it, as if it were a horse of great beauty, then shot it in the head.

Snow had swallowed the road and concealed the deep ravines along its edges, making walking treacherous. Around seven o'clock we spied Aunt Florencia walking with Sergeant Ildefonso. My aunt hugged me and Catalina with all her might, planting kisses on our faces. The sergeant patted my aunt's hand.

"See, there, Florencia. I told you they would be fine."

"Aunt Florencia, where are the girls?" I asked.

"They are with Catalina's grandfather," she replied. "Isn't he with you, dear?" she asked Catalina, her thick brows knit with worry.

Catalina began to tremble. "No...we got separated. Oh, Lorenzo, what are we to do?"

The sergeant's face grew pale. He had not shaved in days, and the stubble made him look like a raggedy bear.

"We will spread out and look for them. Be careful where you step."

Our group separated and began calling the names of the children and Señor Sandoval. As the moments passed, the voices of Catalina and my aunt grew more desperate. The sun had come out and was melting the snow. Slush formed in ruts as men and wagons began moving out. I could not help but wonder if His Excellency had spent a night as cold and miserable as thousands of his troops had.

We were not alone in our search. All around, women and soldiers looked for comrades and family. Soon the air was filled with wails of women who had discovered dead or injured loved ones.

Suddenly I heard a goat's bell clanging. I sighed with relief. The old man and my sisters must have slept with the goats to keep warm. I saw Catalina struggling through knee-high snow toward a ravine where her goats were gathered. She slid down the slope.

"*¡Abuelito!*" she screamed, and fell to her knees in front of a still form that looked like a white statue. She brushed away the snow to reveal a gray face surrounded by a familiar striped *sarape.*

I ran through the snow, with Aunt Florencia, Esteban, and the sergeant not far behind. I dropped beside Catalina, who was sobbing hysterically. Her grandfather was motionless, and a serene beauty had settled over his face, though it was the color of death. I tried to move the old man's hand, to see if there might be a pulse, but his arm was stiff.

Catalina put her head on my chest and sobbed. As I comforted her, I fought back my own tears. I felt guilty for all the things I had said and thought about the old man.

Aunt Florencia reached over and softly touched his cold face.

"A great hero of the Revolution has died this day," she said. She kissed his frozen cheek tenderly, then made the sign of the cross.

A dash of color caught my attention in a clump of shrubs a few paces away. I walked closer and began digging away the snow with trembling hands. When I saw the pure, sweet faces of Dulcinea and Aracelia now turned blue, a great mountain of sadness erupted in my heart, spewing my soul with black sorrow. I began shaking with grief and disbelief. Tears streamed down my face.

When Aunt Florencia saw the bodies, an indescribable sound crawled from her throat, more animal than human.

"No! No!" she screamed to the sky. She dropped to her knees and pulled my sisters' stiff bodies close to hers. "My angels. My beautiful angels. *Dios,* why did you do this?" She rocked and wailed until a crowd gathered around.

General Andrade, who was in charge of the Cavalry Brigade, saw the commotion and came down to investigate. His eyes watered, and he gave the kindest words of sympathy to me, Aunt Florencia, and Catalina. He ordered some soldiers to dig graves and bury Señor Sandoval and my sisters.

By midmorning, dozens of dead—soldiers and civilians alike—rested in shallow graves marked by crossed sticks and little piles of stones. We whispered prayers, then I played my flute with the deepest, most passionate notes I could muster, though I barely managed to get through the songs without choking. As the brigade pulled out, I looked at the three mounds of dirt for the last time. I knew I would never be this way again.

The next day, snow fell without stopping. Catalina tore up her petticoat to make socks for her feet and gave cloth to me for my hands. The sergeant and his small troop of men continued, leaving the cavalry behind, for they had lost many supplies, many horses, mules, and several men, especially those from the warm climates who were not dressed for cold weather.

We marched doubly fast the next few days, stopping for nothing, and caught up with the rest of our brigade. Everyone had suffered from the bitter cold and lost supplies, animals, and dozens of soldiers. The number of dead women and children was not even tallied. Many of those who survived lost fingers and toes to frostbite, especially the innocent children.

Each step that drew us closer to Texas brought new tragedies. Desertions increased, and those not captured and executed were often found murdered by savages. Rations grew more scarce, and at a time when the troops needed nourishment the most to endure the heartless march, we were denied the basics of meat, bread, and water. I was too numb with grief to care about food. At night I ate what Aunt Florencia gave me, but I did not speak. Esteban tried to lift my spirits, but nothing mattered. Only hatred for El Presidente kept me putting one foot in front of the other.

On the eighteenth of February, we began meeting a stream of carts filled with citizens of San Antonio de Béxar and their possessions. They were fleeing that town and seeking refuge with relatives in Mexico in anticipation of the battle to come. Some women were on foot, telling stories of marauding Indians who stole their possessions and horses and killed their men.

The refugees said that most of the *norteamericanos* in town were not the original Texas settlers who had legitimately bought land and worked farms for many years but soldiers of fortune, greedy mercenaries from the United States who had no legal right to be on Mexican soil. They roamed the streets like white-skinned giants, loudly boasting their triumphs over General Cós's army. They held loud *fandangos* nightly with rowdy dancing and harassed the pretty girls endlessly. They were hardly ever seen without a bottle of liquor in their hands.

A great sense of indignation rose up among us. We tightened our belts another notch and threw ourselves wholeheartedly into the march, determined that no foreigners would harass Mexican citizens and steal Mexican lands without a fight. Whenever I felt myself weakening and about to complain, I had only to think of the sweet faces of my sisters and a new wave of determination would lift me onward. I could not let their deaths be in vain.

On February 21, a furious storm full of hail, lightning, and unrelenting rain pounded our backs and faces. Men and women alike trudged through deep mud, which caked the wheels of the supply wagons and artillery caissons. The wheels sank, requiring dozens of soldiers to push them along. Women and girls tied the hems of their skirts into knots to keep them off the ground. Our pace slowed to a snail's crawl.

That night everyone slept in mud, with no water to drink, for there were no creeks. I could not help but think about General Santa Anna and his perfect white trousers. He had left with the vanguard a few days ahead of the cavalry and Zapadores Battalion and had probably missed the blizzard. The fleeing townspeople had passed the general along the road, and by all reckoning he and the vanguard troops would be in Béxar the day after tomorrow.

My brigade arrived at the Río Bravo, or what the *norteamericanos* call the Río Grande, on the twenty-fourth. I stood on the banks, observing the pretty river, wide but shallow and slow moving at this place, curving between boulders and desert hills covered with yucca, cactus, tangy creosote, and sage that had burst into purple blooms from the recent rain.

Women and girls bathed in the cold waters and washed their clothes, leaving them on bushes to dry in the sun. A few months ago, I would have been on my hands and knees hiding behind the bushes, stealing glimpses of their brown bodies, but I was too exhausted to partake in even that small pleasure. And somehow, now, it seemed like a childish thing to do.

I saw Catalina coming from the shore, her cheeks pink from the invigorating bath. She held something in her hands, and as she drew closer, I recognized it as her grandfather's *sarape*. She stopped and her dark, sad eyes looked at me dolefully. I had seen her hardly at all since the death of the old man and my sisters. I almost did not recognize her, for her smile had gone. The fire in her eyes was gone, too, and her shoulders were slumped. I wanted to make her pain go away. But how could I? My own pain filled my heart so that I could not even look at Catalina without thinking of that terrible snowstorm.

That night, exhausted though I was, I could not fall asleep right away. My mind whirred with thoughts of war and death. Though my knapsack was filled with ammunition and supplies related to arms, I had not fired my musket more than twice. It was considered a waste of gunpowder and shot. The troops would learn to shoot when the battle began, according to El Presidente.

I relived the steps to loading the gun—prime the firing pan, drop in some powder, drop in the lead ball with its wadding, tamp it down, cock the hammer, pull the trigger. What if in the heat of battle I forgot the sequence? What if I spilled some powder?—the ball would not travel far enough. What if the flash blinded my eyes?

My mind also struggled with every possible thing that might go wrong between here and San Antonio de Béxar. What if all the cavalry horses died from lack of food and water? What kind of army loses its cavalry before the war is even fought? What if the heavy artillery and the rest of the troops, which were lagging leagues behind because of the rough terrain and mud, never caught up with the rest of the army? What kind of general forces his soldiers to march through impassable terrain, in unfathomable conditions, with little food or water?

Sergeant Ildefonso had said that San Antonio de Béxar lay about nine days away. And between here and there was more barren terrain. How many, I wondered, would survive the march to the Alamo? And if they did survive, what kind of soldiers would they be? Soon I would know the answer, for tomorrow we would cross the Río Bravo and step onto the soil of Texas.

FOURTEEN

■ ■ ■ ■ ■ ■ ■ ■

Tejas

Our troops crossed the Río Bravo without much incident. The infantrymen walked across in waist-deep water, carrying their muskets and knapsacks above their heads. The mules also crossed with their packs intact.

But in spite of the gentle nature of the river at this point, several oxen fell and drowned. Since most of the experienced drivers had deserted, ordinary soldiers had been put in charge of the supply wagons and oxen. They did not have the skill or patience for river crossings and urged the scrawny oxen by prodding them with their bayonets. The beasts, exhausted from the long journey and from lack of food, were too weak. Hitched to the carts, they could not rise up if they fell and several drowned. Because of this carelessness, some carts had to be abandoned and their loads were put on the remaining oxcarts and on the backs of the already overburdened pack mules.

The next evening we pitched camp at a place without water. But to make up for this lack, God sent us an abundance of rabbits. Soldiers caught them with their bare hands, as if catching chickens. I captured four large hares and gave them to Catalina, who prepared two over an open flame and made stew with the others. Though her cooking talents were far inferior to those of Aunt Florencia, I swear I had never eaten a rabbit that tasted so good.

Aunt Florencia had been in the lowest of spirits since the tragic events of the blizzard. She didn't seem interested in cooking or ministering to the sick. She often stared into the distance, with tears rolling down her cheeks. She would repeat the words, "I should have stayed in the village. It is my fault the girls are dead. My fault."

Sergeant Ildefonso visited our campsite every evening and gave my aunt comfort. He gently and respectfully helped her with little chores—chopping wood, fetching water. Their growing fondness for each other was obvious.

Catalina found comfort in knowing that her grandfather had lived a long, meaningful life. And she found comfort in her goats. But, like all the animals, the goats were thin and weak. Out of the dozen she had started with, only six remained. Three had died and three had been stolen.

While we ate, a sudden explosion and burst of flames brought everyone to their feet. Soldiers grabbed their guns; women grabbed the children and ducked behind what they could find. With my heart drumming in my ears, I grabbed my musket. I waited for an officer to cry out commands, expecting to hear that the *norte-americanos* had laid an ambush. But after shouts and cries died down, the all-clear signal came. It had not been an attack at all, but the powder supply of the Aldama Battalion catching on fire due to carelessness.

The sergeant laughed and slapped his knee. His body, once round and shaped like a toad, was now trim, and his once-tight uniform hung loose around the ribs. This was the first time I had seen him laugh since the blizzard. He had felt responsible for the group of men he led. It was a great relief to see his mind on something else for a change.

"The explosion was so loud," Esteban said. He often joined us at night for the evening meal. "Is that what cannons sound like, Sergeant?"

The sergeant chewed his stringy rabbit a bit before answering. "No, *muchacho*, cannon fire has a different sound. There is the explosion, of course, and the flame and the smoke, and the smell of burnt powder. But there is the whine of the ball as it hurls through the air for a few seconds, then a crash as it hits its mark. If the cannon is loaded with grapeshot, there is the cry of dying and wounded men, as pieces of metal rip into their bodies. Once you have heard the sound of cannonade, you will never mistake it for any other."

Esteban put his rabbit down and looked away. His body trembled slightly.

"Do you not like your rabbit?" Catalina asked.

Esteban took another bite, then put the bone down. "It is delicious, Catalina, but I am not hungry. My stomach is queasy. It does not know what to do with so much food at once. I will save it for later."

*** *** ***

The next morning we again encountered so many jackrabbits that we could not help but laugh at their antics as they bounded out of the way, right and left, their huge mulelike ears pointed heavenward, their long back legs carrying them effortlessly across the sage-covered plain.

We marched along single file, in the most disorderly way imaginable. The vanguard of the division with the commander was leagues ahead of the middle, and the middle was leagues ahead of the rear guard where the second-in-command rode. Each section traveled at its own pace, as if it were a small isolated army of its own, unrelated to the others. Mounted couriers carrying messages and orders from one brigade to the next often took a day or more. No one section knew what was happening to the other.

More oxen died, too weary to go on, even though the soldiers pricked them with their bayonets, cracked them with their whips, and shouted until their voices grew hoarse. Oxen that died were not slaughtered for food, for they had no meat on their bones worth the effort. Even buzzards were disappointed.

That day, February 26, our brigade commander received a communication from His Excellency, General Santa Anna, saying he and about one thousand soldiers had arrived at San Antonio de Béxar on the twenty-third. The Texan rebels, hungover from a *fandango* celebrating the birthday of their famous American president George Washington, had barricaded themselves in the old mission fortress *El Alamo*. They had the captured Mexican cannons on the parapets, and no one knew for sure how many rebels were there.

General Santa Anna's orders called for the Aldama and Toluca sappers to start forced marches immediately, under the command of Colonel Duque. The rest of the troops were ordered to remain with General Gaona. Sergeant Ildefonso was assigned to the Toluca sappers and arranged for Esteban and me to come along. He pointed out that I had broad shoulders and had experience digging trenches. I was also an excellent swimmer, able to sound out rivers. And Esteban was a favorite of Santa Anna himself.

Though I was glad to be with the sergeant, who had become like a father to me, not long into the march my legs wished I had stayed behind. My aunt and Catalina, not to mention her goats, could not keep up with our grueling pace. It would probably take days for them to catch up with us.

On the twenty-eighth, we crossed the Nueces River, a narrow and deep stream of great beauty. On a tree to the left of a wooden bridge, people had carved inscriptions. Esteban read them aloud, for like me, most of the conscripts could not read. One carving said: ON THE 16TH OF FEBRUARY 1834 THE FIRST COLONY FROM THE VILLA DE DOLORES PASSED BY HERE. Under this another carving said: ON THE 15TH OF THE SAME MONTH IN 1836 THE FIRST DIVISION OF THE ARMY BOUND FOR TEXAS PASSED.

Esteban scratched his initials and, in an act of friendship, carved mine, too, then added the date. As he did so, a chill ran up my backbone. I imagined children many years in the future pointing and saying: "I wonder who this was, his age, his name, if he lived or died."

The twenty-ninth of February, a leap-year day, found us at a ranch overlooking strikingly beautiful country. The serenity and awe of distant hills combined to form an unforgettable impression. The beauty of nature, however, was soon replaced with her cruelty when we reached the Frio River and a blustery norther chilled us all night long.

Refreshed from drinking all the water we needed, we crossed the Frio River on March 1. The norther continued and snow fell. It grew so cold that night that a young captain who kept a journal could not write because the ink froze in its bottle. Though beautiful, the white flakes only reminded me of Señor Sandoval and my dear sisters.

167

We camped at Arroyo Hondo. I saw wild turkeys—strange-looking animals but delicious when roasted. That night an unfortunate soldier from the Toluca Battalion froze to death and we buried him the next day. Some mules had wandered off in the night, and their packs had to be added to those of the already over-burdened mules remaining.

The deeper we traveled into Texas, the more apprehensive I became. Although Texas was part of Mexico, to most of the soldiers it felt like a foreign land. The *norteamericano* settlers outnumbered the Mexican settlers ten to one. They were white-skinned giants, who forced black-skinned African slaves to work for them in cotton fields. They ate strange foods, wore strange clothes, spoke a foreign language, and were not Catholic.

As we grew closer to Béxar, each soldier pondered if he would be brave or cowardly; would he fight the enemy and gladly give his life for his country or hide and protect his own skin? The experienced soldiers did not seem to think of this, but I was sure that every conscript whispered the same prayer at night: *God, grant me the courage to be brave. God, keep me alive.*

We arrived at the Medina River, a small stream abundant with pecan trees. We ate what good nuts could be found, but I suspected that Ramírez y Sesma's soldiers preceding us had taken most of them. This was the same creek, the sergeant told me, where Spanish soldiers had fought against some rebelling colonists many years ago, while Mexico was still under the Spanish regime. As a young soldier, General Santa Anna had participated in that battle.

That same day our commander received orders from El Presidente. We were to get a good rest before marching into San Antonio de Béxar, less than eight leagues away. A corporal complained of severe pain and groaned loudly all day. There were no doctors or medical supplies to help him, a fact that disturbed Sergeant Ildefonso greatly.

That evening before dark, while making his rounds, the sergeant stopped beside my campfire, which I was sharing with Esteban. In his hands the sergeant held a rolled-up blanket.

"Listen, *muchachos,*" he said, and cupped his hand around his ear. "Do you hear it?"

I strained my ears and heard a dull rumble, like distant thunder.

"What is it?" I asked.

"Cannonade," the sergeant replied. "We are close now. This time tomorrow we will be in Béxar, taking part in the siege. The rebels are barricaded inside that old mission, and our army is hurling cannonballs at them continuously. It would be pointless to fire our muskets at those thick walls. Rumor says a few of our men have been killed, but it is just a matter of time until the victory is ours. The *norteamericanos* will run out of food and ammunition and cannonballs. Sappers will dig trenches so that our men will be protected when they approach. Our cannonballs will pound the mission walls until they cave in. I would not be surprised to learn that they are ready to surrender tomorrow."

"And what if they do not surrender?" Esteban asked.

"Then we will overrun them. But do not worry about that happening yet. The heavy artillery is still a few days behind us. El Presidente will surely wait until it arrives before he plans a final attack. Time is on our side. Now, rest well. In the morning we will put on our full dress uniforms. We must present a solid front to the enemy and let him see that we are united in our cause."

The sergeant unrolled the blanket and shook out a uniform, worn but in good condition. "This is for you," he said, and placed it in my arms.

"Muchas gracias," I said, trying not to act like an excited child at *fiesta* time. I did not ask the sergeant where the uniform came from, for I knew what the answer would be. The groaning of the soldier had stopped, and the blue-and-red coat still showed the outline of a corporal's stripe recently ripped off.

After the sergeant left, Esteban looked at me, his eyes dark and shimmering in the partial light of the moon that had risen.

"I will die there," he said with no emotion.

"Didn't I tell you dreams do not matter?" I tried to joke, but Esteban rolled over and closed his eyes. Soon his breathing grew slow and deep. I envied Esteban's ability to sleep anywhere, anytime, even with thoughts of certain death dancing in his mind.

I rolled on my back and stared at the brilliant stars above. Long after everyone else was asleep, as owls screeched and flew from tree to tree on their silent wings, I thought about what the sergeant had said about putting on uniforms and presenting a solid front. I prayed that the *norteamericanos* did not see our ribs showing through the cloth or the blisters on our feet or the exhaustion in our eyes.

FIFTEEN

San Antonio de Béxar

The next morning, March 3, commenced clear and chilly. I put on the uniform, which fit well, except for the trousers being three inches too long. Those who had them, replaced sandals with shoes or boots. Perhaps we were not a united front, but at least most of us wore the same color.

With each league we marched, the cannonade grew louder. Nervous sweat trickled down my back and temples, though it was a cool day. My heart fluttered as each step brought us closer. All the men marched in silence, each lost in his own thoughts of war and courage and death.

At last we stood on the summit of Alazan Hill and looked down on the little town of San Antonio de Béxar. White houses, a large church, and an old Spanish mission glistened in the sun. The mission—small, square, and ugly—stood across the river from the town in an open field. The cannons mounted on the walls were silent, but smoke rose from the Mexican batteries across the San Antonio River and on the north side of the mission.

"Is that the Alamo?" Esteban asked the sergeant.

"*Sí*. That is where the troublesome rebels are barricaded."

"But it is so small," I protested. "For that little fort El Presidente has gathered the Mexican army? It is like an ant fighting a bull."

"Yes, but remember, if enough ants sting the bull, he will fall," the sergeant said.

Suddenly a boom of cannonade rocked the air and shook the earth, interrupting our conversation. It had come from a large eighteen-pounder mounted on one of the Alamo walls. It was larger than any of the Mexican cannons being fired, for our heavy artillery was still lagging leagues to the south, making its way over the rugged terrain. How ironic, I thought, that the rebels were defending themselves with Mexican cannons captured from General Cós in December.

I felt giddy, and my mouth went dry. The sergeant rode along the line, yelling at the men to straighten their hats, shift their knapsacks, lace their shoes, or wipe the dust from their faces. The bugler blasted the signal to move out and the column surged forward. Down the hill we marched, straight and surefooted, to the beat of the fife and drum, singing songs of war and courage.

As we swarmed into the town, music from a band struck up a lively tune and cannons saluted with booms so loud the horses neighed and reared. Church bells pealed wildly, and I felt as if we were the most important soldiers on the face of the earth.

The town was almost empty, but citizens who had remained waved handkerchiefs and cheered. Women threw flowers at our feet and old men shouted *"¡Viva México!"* As our columns turned down a pleasant tree-lined street, I saw signs of the battle that had taken place in December. Small holes riddled the *adobe* walls, and larger, gaping holes in the doors and roofs showed where cannonballs had struck, or where men had hacked their way from house to house. Some of the homes were quite lovely, others small and neat, their balconies spilling over with colorful flowers.

From a tall church steeple, the Mexican flag and another, blood red in color, waved. The red flag was the symbol of no quarter. When the victory was won, no rebel would be spared. This was the order of El Presidente.

A captain came out to meet the new troops and directed us to the rest of the army. After we were shown where to camp, I learned that the music and cannon fire was not in our honor after all, but to celebrate the victory of General Urrea over some rebels at a settlement in southern Texas called San Patricio. I was very disappointed.

It was late afternoon by the time we arrived, so we pitched our tents and settled in right away. A few of us walked to the San Antonio River to wash our dusty faces and hands. The Alamo stood about one hundred yards away. The buildings were in poor condition. The roof of the chapel was missing, apparently having fallen in years ago. Next to it was a long row of living quarters formerly used by *padres* or Indians, now used as barracks. A Mexican flag with two stars in its center—signifying Coahuila and Texas—instead of the eagle and snake, arrogantly waved from a pole. The ruins of a little village were scattered near the mission. Many wooden *jacales* had been burned by the enemy to keep the Mexican soldiers from using them as cover. A skirmish had occurred there several days ago, and some of our soldiers had been killed by enemy sharpshooters.

I saw a few *norteamericano* sentries staring over the thick walls that surrounded the open plaza of the old mission. They were a raggedy bunch. Their clothing appeared to be mostly deerskin; some even wore animal skins on their heads. They observed in silence from the walls, watching us like hidden rabbits watching wolves. Suddenly a single musket ball whistled through the air and smacked a tree behind us. As we ducked and ran back to our camp, I heard cheers rise from the white walls. The accuracy of the shooter amazed me.

As it grew darker, music started up in a *cantina* down the street, and the laughter of women and men filled the air. It was good to hear it. Perhaps this war would not be so bad after all. If we were fortunate, the *norteamericanos* would surrender without a fight and we could all go home very soon.

Later that night, music from a strange instrument drifted over the mission walls. It sounded like the wailing of a cat, yet it carried a pleasant tune. Then I heard the crisp, clear notes of a fiddle, playing the same tune.

"What a beautiful melody," Esteban said. "I wonder how old the musician is? Do you think there are boys your age inside those walls?"

"I do not think so," I replied. "I have heard they are a volunteer army. What boy in his right mind would join such an army?" I said these words, yet I could not shake the image from my head of a boy, fair of skin, playing a tune, staring across the river at our campfires.

■ ■ ■

March 4 commenced very windy, but warmer than the day before. The Mexican cannons began firing early, so no man could sleep, even if he had permission to. In spite of the cannonade, the enemy did not fire back, except for the eighteen-pounder, which fired once a day. The sergeant said it was a signal to the Texan colonies that the Alamo was still held by *norteamericanos.*

Overnight the enemy had sallied out and fought a skirmish at an old sugar mill. The enemy's supplies were low and whenever possible they tried to steal food from houses in the town. The Mexican soldiers did some stealing of their own. I heard that a party of our men confiscated corn and cattle from *tejano* ranchers who sympathized with the rebels.

During the day, high-ranking officers from all the battalions gathered at His Excellency's new headquarters. His old headquarters had been blasted by the big rebel cannon only three days before. I overheard voices arguing as they discussed when to assault the Alamo. Some wanted to wait for the twelve-pound cannons that were still three days' journey away. Others wanted to assault the old mission immediately.

I loitered outside the building, keeping my ear as close to the window as possible. A captain yanked me away. I think I would have been shot if I had not shown him the note I always carried from El Presidente. When General Santa Anna saw me, he greeted me kindly and said he hoped to hear my flute again soon. The captain ordered me to get to work on sapper detail.

A short time later, I found myself in mud and cold water, digging a trench in what had once been an aqueduct leading to the mission. We dug all night like desperate moles, and by dawn we had almost reached the Alamo's outer wall. Some sentries above saw us and fired a few shots. A bullet grazed the man next to me, drawing blood, but by that time the work was done. That night I had only three hours of sleep.

March 5 began very mild and clear. I was pleased to

learn that the lagging women had arrived. I greeted Aunt Florencia with open arms. Catalina was long-faced because more of her goats had been stolen.

"Without my goats, I am nothing," she cried. "Who will marry a goatherd who has no goats? I swear that I will kill the next soldier who tries to steal one of my goats!"

Ah, how wonderful her angry voice sounded. I was relieved to see that her deep grief had yielded to anger. The old Catalina was back. I had not realized until that moment how much I missed her complaining. Now, for at least a while, the world seemed right again.

I could not help but notice that Sergeant Ildefonso's eyes twinkled when he saw Aunt Florencia again. He removed his hat and bowed like a gentleman. She smiled lightly and let him kiss her hand. Well, I had heard of miracles, so why not let the sergeant believe he could win her heart?

The north battery commenced a brisk fire at the enemy, but they did not respond. The sergeant said the men in the Alamo were obviously conserving ammunition. The sergeant's biggest fear was that the rebels would be reinforced any day. About thirty Texans had managed to slip by the Mexican picket lines on March 1 and join the rebels inside the Alamo. For that reason, sentinels were posted on all the roads leading out of town. But at night, it was difficult to see any approaching troops. Rumors flew that four hundred *norteamericano* reinforcements were coming from a town to the south called Goliad. Other rumors claimed that the government of the United States was sending warships to the Gulf loaded with armies. No one knew what to believe.

Later in the day, Esteban and I walked to the corral. I was grooming the sergeant's red horse, which had miraculously managed to survive the long trek from San Luis Potosí, when the sergeant appeared. His face was serious and his lips turned down.

"What is wrong?" Esteban asked.

"Orders have just come from His Excellency. We attack the Alamo tomorrow morning. We will spend the rest of today preparing for battle, and then retire early. The muster will occur at one o'clock and we will attack just before dawn."

"But the heavy artillery hasn't arrived yet," Esteban exclaimed.

The sergeant made the sign of the cross. "Say your prayers and your good-byes, *muchachos*. May God help us all."

SIXTEEN

Dawn at the Alamo

Word of the impending battle spread throughout the encampment like a summer brushfire on the desert. It was almost with relief that men threw themselves into the preparation, glad at last for the end of the thirteen-day siege.

Each infantryman was given a pickax for breaking in doors and walls and a hook for grappling over the mission walls. Men made scaling ladders by binding strong sticks of wood with rawhide. We received our ration of cartridges and flints. Each man was ordered to wear his shoes or sandals. There were to be no bare feet. No one was allowed to wear his cloak, long coat, *sarape,* or *manga* on his shoulders, for fear that it might get caught on something and interfere with the forward rush. Soldiers who carried ladders, twenty-eight of them in all, were told to sling their muskets over their shoulders so that they could easily carry the ladders to the appointed places.

All afternoon the sound rose through the encampment of men cleaning their muskets and packing their cartridge boxes and cavalrymen preparing their saddles and mounts. All the while the battery along the northern wall continued firing cannonade at the old mission.

I prepared my musket, carefully cleaning the residue from the barrel, then lightly oiling it. I cleaned the firing pan and replaced the flint. Like all the soldiers, I had been given seventy cartridges, more than enough to win the day, for battles were often won with only a few volleys of gunfire.

The cannons stopped firing at dusk, and the soldiers retired early. I saw men saying good-bye to their families and friends and making their last wishes known. I saw them kneeling in prayer. I said good-bye to Aunt Florencia and gave her my flute, in case I did not return. I did not see Catalina.

Some Indians who camped near my tent did not eat. When I asked one why, he said that it helped in case of stomach wounds. The thought of an injury in the stomach made my blood turn cold. I had heard that men wounded in an arm or leg could be saved by amputation, but a man hit in the stomach could only be left to die a slow, miserable death.

The silence was eerie. When the sergeant came for a final check, he stopped and sat down. He looked at the fort for a long time before speaking, then he looked directly at me.

"His Excellency has ordered you to stay behind with the musicians and the reserves. After all, he cannot let his favorite flute player get killed, eh?" The sergeant smiled. "For once I agree with the general; you are too young." He turned his gaze to Esteban, who sat up, his dark eyes burning.

"I do not want to stay with the reserves," Esteban said. "I want to fight."

The sergeant nodded. "I know, *muchacho*. I will try to watch out for you." He looked across the river at the Alamo again and spoke, more to the air than to us: "I have an uneasy feeling about this battle. I heard a dog howling under my bed last night." His words came from an old song about a dying man. It was a thing to say when you had a premonition about dying.

I grabbed the sergeant's arm. "No, Sergeant Ildefonso, do not say that. They are just a small band of rebels. The battle cannot take more than a few moments. I heard Colonel Duque say that."

The sergeant forced a dry smile. "Of course, you are right. I am being foolish. We will fight for the glory of Mexico and show those mercenaries that they cannot insult our country and our people by stealing our land." He rose, tugging at his coatee.

"Promise me one thing, *muchacho*," he said to Esteban. "There is no hospital; there are no doctors. Those with wounds will die a long and painful death. If I am severely wounded, put a gun to my head and let me die with dignity. It is all I ask." He did not wait for Esteban's answer, but hurried away on his short legs toward Aunt Florencia's camp. I imagined they would have a sad farewell.

After the sergeant left, Esteban rose and put on his boots. "I am going to the latrine," he said, then slipped into the darkness.

Left alone, I knelt beside my bedding and placed a small wooden cross on the blanket. I whispered a prayer to Mother Mary, Sweet Jesus, and God Himself. I crossed myself and curled up on my *petate* and pulled my blanket over my shoulders. They felt bony to the touch.

The murmur of praying voices drifted over the encampment. I wished there were priests about, but in addition to the hospital, food, and uniforms, priests were another thing that His Excellency had forgotten to bring along.

I was almost asleep when I heard a scraping noise. I opened my eyes and saw Catalina standing a few feet away.

"Were you not going to say good-bye to me?" she said with a challenge in her voice.

I sat up. "I do not like tearful farewells. I want to remember you the way you are, not as a whimpering, crying girl."

"What makes you think I would cry for you?" She put her hands on her hips, no longer plump but narrow in spite of the layers of clothes.

When I did not reply, she sat beside me. "I brought something for you," she said softly. She opened her hand, revealing a rosary made from colored yarn and round seeds.

I touched the smooth seeds, imagining the hours she had put into making it, the gathering of seeds along the long journey, tirelessly stringing them with a needle made from the thorn of an *agave*.

"*Muchas gracias*, Catalina," I said. "It is a fine rosary— the best I've ever owned." As I slipped it around my neck, I noticed that she held another one in her hand. She followed my gaze.

"I made a rosary for Esteban, too." She smiled lightly. "He is a haughty *criollo*, but sometimes he be- haves like a normal human. Please give it to him for me. I will pray for you, Lorenzo Bonifacio," she said, turning her liquid-brown eyes toward me. "I will pray for all of you." She leaned over before I could stop her and placed a soft kiss on my lips. Before I could respond, she spun on her heels and ran into the darkness. I felt guilty for not telling her I had been ordered to stay behind.

▰ ▰ ▰

I had hardly fallen asleep when something jarred me awake. The sergeant was walking up and down the com- pany line, whispering and shaking shoulders, rousing every man. The moon was up, but clouds scudded past it.

Esteban rubbed his eyes. "What time is it?" he whispered.

"One o'clock," someone whispered back.

Esteban was wearing the rosary that I had given him last night after he returned. I could not help but smile. Four months ago he would have scoffed at such a humble, plainly made piece of work. It occurred to me at that moment that I actually liked Esteban Esquivel.

General Santa Anna had divided his army into four columns, one for each side of the Alamo. Esteban would go with the sergeant to the column led by Colonel Duque. I was to stay with the musicians and the Zapadores Battalion, who remained with General Santa Anna safely behind the lines. The Zapadores would be called to fight only if the other four columns were driven back.

In all there were about fourteen hundred men in the columns, and four hundred in reserve. The rawest conscripts, who had no guns, would not be used. But even those who had been in the army for months, like me, had not been trained. The cannons were to remain silent during the battle, for fear of hitting our own soldiers.

The darkness made it difficult to see what we were doing, but all around I heard the soft rustle of cloth and the click of equipment. Because Santa Anna wanted to take the fort by surprise, no fires were allowed. Men could not even smoke their cigarettes. Were it not for the occasional glimpse of moonlight striking silver bayonets and the white hats that all officers were instructed to wear, I would not have been able to see the creeping columns.

At three o'clock the columns crossed the San Antonio River, two abreast. Their shoes made soft padding noises on the wood planks of the footbridge. Each column settled in its station, each one approximately one hundred *varas* from the white fort.

My heart ached with remorse that I was not part of it. I should have gone on my knees and kissed El Presidente's feet for holding me back, but I resented being considered too young to put up a good fight. After all, I had fired my musket two times, more than some of the other men creeping to their posts.

As the sappers and musicians positioned themselves behind Santa Anna, who straddled his fine white horse, a sudden urge swept over me. I would not stay behind like a useless child. I had made the march of death and survived. I was a man and I would prove it. When the general turned his head, I stooped low and ran toward Colonel Duque's column, assigned to the north wall.

Under the cover of darkness, I slipped into the column unnoticed and sat on the ground with the silent men. It was too dark to see the faces, but I knew that Esteban was nearby. The night air was cold and the ground was colder still. I began to shiver, wishing I had my *sarape*.

Someone whispered that it was four o'clock and that we would have at least an hour to wait before attacking. I recognized the voice of a young man from my village named Hector, a great trickster. Hector joked about his fingers being too cold to pull the trigger of his musket. I tried to laugh, but my throat would not move. The sergeant hushed Hector, and it grew quiet again.

Silence settled down on the columns of men. No one spoke, but frosty breath came from every man's mouth. Some closed their eyes and went back to sleep; others removed their *shakos*, which were cumbersome with their tall tops and pressing chin straps. A few moved their lips in silent prayer and fingered their rosary beads. I could not help but wonder which of us would lie silent in a pool of blood in only a short while. Who would lose an arm? A leg? Whose life would be ruined? Who would become a hero?

The time passed painfully slow. I wanted to shift positions more often, but each time I did, a belt buckle, bayonet, or cartridge box clinked. The man next to me began to snore so loudly that I was afraid the enemy sentries would hear. When someone whispered that it was five o'clock, I could not believe that only one hour had passed.

I wished I could find Esteban and Sergeant Ildefonso, but I dared not move about. I stared at the sinking moon, half-hidden by thin clouds. It reminded me of the times when I lay on the flat roof of our *adobe* hut, staring at the moon or stars, or sleeping among the ears of corn drying in the hot sun. I often had dreamed of getting away from that miserable little village, of going to places far away with interesting buildings and strange plants. Now I was in such a place, and all that I could think of was getting home alive and sitting on the roof in the drying corn.

A noise jolted me out of my dream, and I realized I had dozed off for a moment. The eastern sky was turning the slightest shade of gray, but it was still dark around the mission.

"It is time," Colonel Duque whispered, as he slipped on his officer's hat. I was surprised to see that the colonel had been only a few feet away.

Lieutenant Ochoa walked among the men, whispering, "Fix bayonets! Ready your weapons!"

Clicking noises ran along the column, as men fastened their bayonets to the muzzles of their guns and cocked hammers.

"We must surprise the enemy," the lieutenant continued. "Do not talk or shout. Do not fire until you are almost at the wall. Remember to fire from the shoulder, not from the hip, even though the kick may make you think your shoulder is going to fall off." He paused a moment.

"We fight for the glory of Mexico, to drive out these rebel thieves who have stolen our lands and murdered our comrades. We must avenge our fallen brothers. We will fight until every man is killed. Remember, show no quarter."

His voice faded into the night and my lips began to move: *Hail Mary, full of grace, the Lord is with thee; blessed are thou among women, and blessed is the fruit of thy womb, Jesus. Holy Mary, Mother of God, pray for us sinners, now and at the hour of our death. Amen. Hail Mary, full of grace...*

"Ready! Arms!" The lieutenant's loud whisper cut into my prayer.

I shifted my musket to a charging position. The barrel felt icy cold, sending a shiver down my already trembling body. My heart began pumping furiously.

It is going to happen. It is going to happen now. This moment. This second.

SEVENTEEN

■ ■ ■ ■ ■ ■ ■ ■ ■

Victory
or Death!

A shrill bugle charge cut into the chilly air. With shouts from sergeants and lieutenants and captains, the four columns surged toward the white walls like four black serpents. From behind the lines, a band of drums and fifes struck up and the trumpets blared *el degüello*, a fast, rousing tune that reminded me of Spain and bullfights, and death.

The enemy awakened, shouting in their strange language. "Mexicans! Mexicans! *Gautdamyee!*" they screamed.

We ran in the darkness over the one hundred *varas*, across the open field. Part of Duque's columns foolishly broke the command of silence, with shouts of *"¡Viva México! ¡Viva Santa Anna!"* and fired too soon, in spite of orders.

The enemy responded to the noise and musket flashes with deadly gunfire and a cannon filled with grapeshot. It struck the middle of the Toluca Battalion and cut down half their experienced chasseurs. Screams from the dying and wounded burned my ears.

A cannonball whistled through Duque's column, knocking off everything it hit—arms, legs, heads—and cutting bodies in half as it coursed through the ranks. I saw the pumpkin head of Lieutenant Ochoa roll across the ground in front of me, its white hat now red with blood. Vomit surged up my throat and spilled down the front of my uniform and onto the ground. My legs turned to water, and I shook so violently that only running kept me standing.

The sounds of my pounding heart in my ears and the shouts of men and the blasts of muskets and cannons were so loud that I could not hear the drum signals or the officers' shouts. I followed what the men around me did, not knowing where I was going or what was happening.

On all sides, fire and smoke spat from musket muzzles. The Alamo walls lit up like a lightning strike each time the enemy fired cannons and a rifle volley. *Norteamericanos* along the walls aimed with deadly precision, seeming to have many weapons each. A soldier in front of me screamed, clutched his neck, and fell over. Blood gushed between his fingers as he writhed in pain, unable to speak, for his vocal cords had been blown away.

The Texan cannons boomed like thunder, shelling their deadly shrapnel into our ranks, cutting down thirty men at a time. I ran faster toward the north wall, stopping only to fire and reload. The flash from my musket blinded my eyes and the acrid taste of gunpowder filled my mouth. Once, as I grappled to load my gun, my fingers shook so violently that I dropped the paper cartridge. As I stooped to retrieve it, a musket ball buzzed over my head and struck the man behind me with a sickening wet slap. I heard a cry and the gurgle of blood, then silence. I reloaded my gun and fired again at the silhouettes on top of the wall.

I screamed like a madman as my column ran forward, fighting against the barrage of grapeshot, the deadly rebel rifles, and the growing light. As I staggered along, my eyes stinging from smoke, a man near me fell face forward. I saw a bullet hole in the man's back. Then another man fell, a hole in his back also.

"*¡Dios mío!*" a captain shouted. "The other column is shooting us!" He screamed and waved his white hat to get the attention of the soldiers behind us, but a bullet caught him in the chest.

Our column veered to one side to avoid the fire coming from our own troops, only to be barraged by the rebels. So it was with all the columns. They fell back, then charged forward again. So great was the confusion that three of the columns ran into each other, mingling until no one knew his unit sergeant or his captain or his general. I saw Colonel Duque fall, a hideous wound in his leg. His men trampled over him, but still he shouted orders from the ground until one of his officers helped him up.

The fifteen minutes that had gone by felt like an eternity. Time seemed suspended as I worked my way to the wall. Men huddled against it, their chests heaving as they gasped for air. The enemy's cannon sitting only a few feet above our heads could not swivel down to fire upon us. We fired up as the rebels fired down. We waited for the soldiers with ladders who had been assigned to this wall.

"Where are the damned ladders?!" a sergeant yelled, just before a bullet hit his arm. We waited, but no ladders came. Without the ladders, we could not scale the steep wall.

Suddenly a bullet whizzed past my ear and chipped the wall. Then another bullet thudded the wall. The next grazed my arm, cutting through the cloth, leaving a red gash. I squinted across the smoky field I had just crossed and saw the four hundred reserve units running toward the mission, shouting and firing. They were aiming so badly they were missing the top of the wall and hitting the soldiers below. Men began to fall around me.

"Forget the ladders!" I shouted. I ducked and ran to another group of soldiers pressed against the wall; I arrived at the same moment as five soldiers with ladders.

Eager to be the first up the wall, five ambitious soldiers grabbed the ladders and scaled them, only to be stabbed or shot as soon as they reached the top. The rebels pushed the ladders down. But that did not stop us. Others took up the ladders and continued the assault;

each time men were killed and the ladders were thrown back, until the pile of dead soldiers at the foot of the wall was layers deep. So many incensed soldiers tried to scale the ladders at the same time, the wooden rungs broke into bits.

As one ladder after another broke, and as the pile of dead soldiers grew larger, I began to give up hope that we would ever get over the wall. A sergeant grabbed a hatchet and began hacking at the wall itself. Another soldier used his pick like a grapple to climb up the wall. Now, with the reserves mingling with the four columns, hundreds of soldiers were pushing, attempting to climb the north wall, which had been weakened by thirteen days of bombardment. In a place where it had been repaired, we found gaps and toeholds, which served as a crude ladder.

With screams rattling in their throats, soldiers poured over the breach, flying and falling and stumbling like a herd of stampeding cattle going over a canyon wall. The enemy, seeing that they were overwhelmed, fled their posts at the wall and retreated to the open plaza, firing into the hoard of rushing soldiers. Some rebels sought shelter in rows of small *adobe* buildings that had once served as housing for the mission *padres*. The rebels had already cut out slots in the walls earlier and now fired from them with deadly accuracy.

My captain had instructed us to reserve our ammunition for distance firing, and to use only bayonets in close combat, but many of the soldiers now forgot their instructions and fired at the enemy, only to miss and hit their comrades. Even though the dawn had broken and a pale light filled the plaza, so thick was the smoke that no man could see the uniform of the man a few feet away. Some fired wildly at anything that moved.

A few minutes later, our soldiers seized the Texans' eighteen-pounder and turned it on the enemy, smashing their other cannons and bombarding walls. Fires broke out all around us.

Inside the plaza, men fought bravely hand to hand. When the rebels ran out of ammunition, they used knives, or rifle butts, or their fists. I had fired dozens of times at the Alamo but did not know if I had struck a man or not. I would have to use my bayonet soon.

I felt numb, like a man risen from the dead as I pushed forward. The smoke was so thick I almost did not see the rebel a few feet away, leaning on a wall. The rebel was wounded, his right arm dangling from his body. His hair was a rusty brown, and two large blue eyes stared at me from a face blackened with soot and gunpowder. I was suddenly filled with hatred. I ran at the rebel, screaming at the top of my lungs, "I'll kill you! I'll kill you!"

The rebel opened his mouth and whispered words in a strange language. He held his blood-covered hand up in a weak defense and slumped down the wall, trembling.

Suddenly I realized he was a mere boy, no more than fourteen. Remorse swept over me and bitter tears stung my eyes.

I wanted to ask the boy what he was doing here mixed up with these insurgents. I wanted to ask him if he had been dragged from the fields and forced to fight as I had been. From the puddle of blood on the youth's chest and on the ground near him, I knew he would die soon. What did it matter if he was given a few more minutes of life? I lowered my bayonet and walked away. A sharp cry made me turn around. A corporal's bayonet had pierced the boy's heart, and he now sat motionless, his blue eyes staring up, his mouth open wide.

The sound of gunfire began to die down. Some of the rebels hoisted little white flags out of the holes in the barrack walls, some even used their socks. But when my comrades approached, rebels shot them down. This caused a new wave of rage and vengeance.

Driven to near insanity with battle rage, some soldiers stabbed their bayonets into the rebels again and again. Although the rebels tried to beg for mercy, speaking Spanish with heavy accents hard to understand, the soldiers ran them through with steel mercilessly.

■ ■ ■

In what seemed like an eternity and no time at all, the battle was over. A few rebels were still holed up in the barracks, but we were victorious. I leaned against a wall to catch my breath. I heard a groan and saw a man move on the ground a few feet away. In the thick smoke, I could not tell who it was.

"Lorenzo," the man whispered. The face was black with soot and powder. The right leg was covered with blood and the kneecap was blown apart. Blood covered the man's stomach and chest. With horror, I suddenly recognized what was left of Sergeant Ildefonso. I rushed over and dropped to my knees.

"Your gun," the sergeant pleaded in a strained voice. "Use your gun." His eyes shimmered with pain.

I began to choke. "I—I cannot," I stammered. "You are only wounded—maybe the doctors—"

"There are no doctors!" the sergeant hissed between gritted teeth. "No hospital." He lifted a bloody hand and grasped my sleeve. "Please, do not let Florencia see me like this. Please, use your gun."

I stood. Slowly I cocked the hammer. The sergeant closed his eyes and his lips moved as he said a prayer. Hot tears burned my eyes and rolled down my soot-covered cheeks. A lump as sharp as a knife cut into my throat, and I could not swallow it down. I lowered the barrel to the sergeant's head. I tried to squeeze the trigger, but could not.

I was overcome with shame. "I can't. I can't. Please forgive me," I sobbed, and lowered the muzzle.

An older soldier stopped beside us. He leaned over and whispered to the sergeant, then nodded. He took the musket from my hand and put the barrel to the sergeant's head. Quickly he made the sign of the cross, then pulled the trigger. I dropped to my knees and took the sergeant's limp hand in mine.

"Was he your father?" the man asked, placing a firm but gentle hand on my shoulder. His face and uniform were covered with soot and blood.

I shook my head. "No, this man was my sergeant, but he treated me like a son."

"Is his family traveling with the women?"

"There is a woman who loves him."

"Tell her he died a brave man. I saw him fighting the enemy and saving the lives of several men. He is a true hero. Tell her his dying words were of his love for her." He removed a tiny crucifix from the sergeant's neck. "I think she would like to have this as a memento of her beloved." He pressed it into my hand, then stood. He was very tall. "Are you all right? How old are you?"

"I am fifteen."

The man shook his head and furrowed his brow. "I pray my son never has to go through what you just have. Don't feel remorseful because you could not put the poor sergeant out of his misery. It shows that you are still a human."

"But you did. You, a total stranger, did for him what I, who loved him, could not."

"It is only because I am a stranger that I could do it,"

the man replied. "The battle is over. Return to your unit as soon as you can. Try to put this behind you."

■ ■ ■

As it grew lighter, the sounds of gunfire came only sporadically, with an occasional shout as a rebel was rousted from his hiding place. Daylight brought with it the most grotesque scene imaginable to human eyes. Blood covered the ground of the plaza and had splashed on the white stones of the walls. Around every cannon, piles of dead slumped. In the plaza hundreds of dead Mexicans and rebels lay in grotesque positions. Body parts were scattered everywhere. Some of the dead had caught fire, sending up the awful stench of burning cloth and hair and flesh. Nearly all of the rebels had been stripped, their clothing and possessions taken, leaving their husky white forms exposed. Most looked like young men, only in their twenties.

By six-thirty it was all over. The battle had taken an hour, though it felt like it had lasted half a day. It was hard to believe that the sun had just risen. The faces of the dead Mexican soldiers were covered with black soot and gunpowder, so that they were unrecognizable.

But even more sickening than the dead were the wounded. The soldiers writhed in pain, many unable to get to their feet. They cried for water, for priests, and for death. I wanted to wretch again, but my stomach was empty.

As the smoke cleared and it was safe to walk about, soldiers began searching for their comrades, for their brothers, cousins, fathers, or sons. Women crept on their knees among the dead, washing the faces, looking for their loved ones. Soon cries of anguish blended with the groans of the dying and wounded, interrupted by an occasional shout of jubilation as friends were reunited.

I saw El Presidente ride into the plaza, accompanied by Señor Ruiz, *alcalde* of the town. General Santa Anna wore his campaign uniform of white pants, blue waist sash, long-tailed dark coat, and bi-corn hat.

El Presidente walked among the dead, asking the *alcalde* to identify some of the more famous of the rebels. The commander of the rebels, the one called Travis, had fallen beside a cannon on the north wall, a single bullet in his forehead. He was a handsome man with reddish blond hair and a fine physique. Then Santa Anna was shown the body of the one called James Bowie, who had been married to the daughter of the governor of Coahuila y Texas. For all his reputation as a famous fighter and the inventor of the large knife that bore his name, he had died in his bed, too sick from disease to move.

A few *tejanos* from Béxar had joined forces with the rebels, and their bodies now lay in pools of blood. How sad, I thought, that they chose the side of the rebels. Had they been loyal to Mexico, they would be alive and safe in their homes.

El Presidente was observing the carnage when an

old general named Castrillón led out seven rebel prisoners, men who had managed to survive the battle un-
scathed. One of them was an older man of about fifty,
dressed in buckskins. The old general spoke eloquently
on behalf of the prisoners, asking El Presidente to spare
their lives, to use them as messengers to send word of
the futility of resistance back to the colonies. But El
Presidente grew furious that the old officer had dis-
obeyed his orders of no quarter.

"I told you to take no prisoners!" His Excellency
shouted. He turned to the nearest company of sappers
and screamed, "Kill them!"

Neither officers nor privates moved, for they could
not believe the orders. These rebels, who had fought so
gallantly, deserved mercy. To kill a man in the heat of
battle was self-defense, but to kill unarmed prisoners
was murder. Every soldier felt that way. At that moment
I hated El Presidente with all my heart.

The men who refused probably would have been
made prisoners and executed for treason had not several of the unsoiled officers jumped at El Presidente's
orders and slain the defenseless rebels with gusto. The
unfortunate *norteamericanos* died courageously, even
though they were tortured with knives and bayonets.
After this, all I wanted was to turn away from the blood
and stench.

Soon afterward, I noticed soldiers leading women
and children from the wreckage of the Alamo chapel. All

of the women except one were *tejanas*. The one white female was young and pretty, with black hair and intense blue eyes. She carried a little girl of exceptional beauty in her arms. With her was the black slave of one of the dead rebels. The sight of the women, in their dirty, soot-covered clothes with their frightened eyes and trembling arms, struck a chord of compassion in my heart. I was so grateful that they had been spared that tears welled in my eyes. Thank heavens, El Presidente had the decency to treat the women with courtesy.

The sun was well up now, and some citizens of San Antonio de Béxar came with *carretas*. Conscripts began loading corpses of Mexican soldiers on the carts to haul them to the cemetery. The bodies of the rebels were dragged aside to an area outside the mission a little distance away.

I began searching for Esteban. Every time I saw a dead body with boots, I rushed to it and wiped the face with my sleeve to better see the features. Women came with buckets of water, not only to give to the wounded but to wash the faces of the dead. Some of the severely wounded were put in carts and taken to town, but without doctors or medicine, their fates were sealed.

The sight of the weeping women and children as they found their husbands or sons, fathers or lovers, was heart-wrenching. I could not bear to stay, yet I knew I had to face Aunt Florencia and tell her about Sergeant Ildefonso.

When I finally saw my aunt, she ran toward me, then stopped.

"Lorenzo?"

"*Sí,*" I replied. "I am alive."

She threw her arms around me and squeezed with all her might.

"Thanks to God for sparing your life. And young Esteban?" She pushed herself away and wiped at her red eyes.

"I have not seen him yet. I do not know his fate."

She sighed. "I will help you look for him. My sergeant will be looking, too, I am sure. He took such a liking to Esteban." She smiled weakly.

I swallowed and drew in a deep breath. "Aunt Florencia...the sergeant..."

A cloud passed over her face. Her brow furrowed and her eyes turned wild like those of a captured deer. She shook her head and stepped back.

"No, no, *señor.* You are mistaken." She forced a smile. "The good sergeant is not dead. He is not." She stomped her foot. "Do you know we got married last night?" She tossed her head and laughed. "Can you believe I love that bear of a man?"

"Aunt Florencia, I am sorry," I said softly, and took her hand. I noticed a small gold band on her wedding finger. "He was like a father to me. Come, let me show you where he is."

Aunt Florencia clenched her teeth and jerked her hand free.

"If you are lying, Lorenzo Bonifacio, I will kill you with my bare hands."

I led her to the place where I had left the sergeant, but his body had been moved. In the plaza were carts piled high with limp, blood-soaked corpses of Mexican soldiers. The thought of searching through them sickened me.

"You have to believe me," I said. "He died in my arms. He said to tell you he loved you. And he wanted you to have this." I took the bloodstained crucifix from my pocket. The sight of it struck my aunt like a club. Her face churned with emotion, and she dropped to her knees. She slammed her fist into her skirt with dull thuds. Tears rained down her cheeks. I knelt beside her and placed a hand on her shoulder. I expected her to shrug it off, but she did not resist.

"I have nothing, nothing. I am alone again," she cried, as she swayed from side to side. "Another husband taken by war."

Sobs wracked my aunt's body for a few moments more, then subsided. She ran her sleeve across her nose as she stood.

"Damn Santa Anna and his war," she said, her black eyes fixed on El Presidente, as he strode among the bodies, pointing at cannons and discussing tactics of war with his lackey generals. "Why couldn't it have been he who died instead of my sergeant? I will put a curse on

Santa Anna that God Himself cannot remove." She spat and ground the ball of spit with her heel.

I did not say a word, for what was there to say?

"I must find his body," she said at last. "I cannot bear to let it end without seeing him one final time. Where will the soldiers be buried?"

"I have heard that the Mexican soldiers will be buried in the *camposanto*. But the *norteamericanos* will have no such honor. I saw a wagon leaving not long ago to gather wood for a funeral pyre. Their corpses will be burned like diseased cattle."

"Good," Aunt Florencia said, then spat again. "Those dogs who murdered my sergeant do not deserve a Christian burial. They caused this war and this suffering with their greed. I hope they all burn in the everlasting inferno."

I stayed silent. Nothing I said would bring the sergeant back. Perhaps her hatred for the *norteamericanos* would help to ease the loss.

Suddenly, I wanted Esteban to be alive more than anything. I needed to know that at least one person I knew had not died. With great dread, I turned toward the town, where the wounded were being taken.

EIGHTEEN

A Small Affair

Time seemed to stand still as I wandered through the plaza and outside the walls searching for Esteban. The sight of the dead was gruesome, but the sight of wounded men in the throes of pain was worse.

I was forced to stop my search when His Excellency ordered the troops to muster to hear his victory speech and for a roll call so that a tally of dead and wounded could be estimated. I heard there were about six hundred dead Mexicans. The wounded—many with shattered limbs, holes in their chests or bellies—would die within hours or a few days. Those unable to walk were being carried off by friends to houses in the town. Of course, there were no beds for them. They were put on the hard dirt floors to suffer in the cold and darkness.

Standing in line I looked in dismay at the shambles of my unit. Over half of my company was missing, and some of those assembled were wounded. After a rousing speech from El Presidente, which was greeted with half-hearted *vivas,* the captains began to call roll. Lieutenant Ochoa was dead. Sergeant Ildefonso was dead. Colonel Duque was wounded. Twenty-five Mexican officers had been killed and many others wounded, probably because their tall, plumed hats had made them easy targets.

When the captain called out the name Esteban Esquivel, no one answered. A sickening feeling crept over me, yet I did not give up hope. There was so much confusion, that in spite of the call to assembly, many men were still wandering about, dazed and lost. And the wounded were still being carried away. I was determined that I would find Esteban, if for no other reason than to whisper a prayer over his remains.

After muster I searched the old mission, overturning one gruesome discovery after another. The naked rebel bodies had been dragged to a spot of level ground and placed on a large funeral pyre constructed of alternating layers of wood and corpses. During the fury of battle, I could have sworn there were at least five hundred of the enemy, but after counting, the tally came to about two hundred. Many officers complained among themselves that no general in his right mind would have sacrificed so many of his soldiers for such a small victory. Nothing had been gained. Santa Anna himself, while commenting to an officer, said, "Much blood has been shed; but the battle is over. It was but a small affair."

I overheard an officer complaining about the losses. He then said, "Another victory such as this, and we will lose the war."

The funeral pyre was lit, and soon the air was filled with billowing gray and black smoke. The fat of the ignited bodies crackled in the most disgusting way, and the stench of burning hair and flesh choked my lungs. The whole scene was more sickening than the most frightening nightmare any man could conjure. I felt my stomach churning and had to leave.

I crossed the bridge over the San Antonio River. I saw Catalina immediately, her colorful skirt spread out around her as she knelt beside the small river. Perhaps she was washing her hands or face in the cold water, I thought. But as I came closer I realized what she was looking at. The cemetery had no more room, so the corpses of dozens of Mexican soldiers had been tossed in the river and were floating down its gentle course. Bodies had snagged under the bridge and were piling up there. I ran to Catalina and grabbed her arm.

"No, no, you shouldn't be here," I said, as I gently pulled her up. "This is no place for a girl."

She turned, her face as gray as death. When she saw me, her eyes filled with tears. "Lorenzo," she whispered in a hoarse voice. "You are alive. I was looking for you here..."

She put her arms around my waist and pressed her cheek against my chest. She sobbed bitterly, and I did not try to stop her but put my arms around her shoulders and held with all my might. Later I might have to explain my actions, but it did not matter for now. For this moment we were grieving together for the soldiers we knew and for those we did not know, for the tragedy of human folly. We were the victors of the battle, but I felt no glory, no pride.

"How can they do this?" Catalina said, as she pulled away and turned toward the river. "These soldiers gave their lives, and now they are thrown aside like dead rats. I have not heard one bugle sound in their honor nor heard a priest whisper a prayer. The only ones who seem to care are the women and fellow comrades."

I pulled her away from the water, noticing that it had turned pink from the blood. An older soldier was leaning over the bridge with a long-handled hoe, poking at the bodies, trying to dislodge the one causing the jam. I recognized the face of one of the dead men floating by, a man I had eaten with many times. A man who loved to make others laugh. Now his face was contorted and twisted; from this moment forward I knew I would only remember the man's final fate and not his wit.

When the older soldier on the bridge turned, I saw it was the same man who had ended the suffering of Sergeant Ildefonso.

"Who is that soldier?" Catalina asked, pointing at the man on the bridge.

"I do not know," I replied.

"He has a very familiar look. I think I have met him before."

"I must speak to him about the sergeant."

"Is Sergeant Ildefonso dead, too?" Her eyes looked into mine, and I felt as if a knife had stabbed my heart.

"*Sí,*" I said softly. "That soldier on the bridge may know where he is buried."

We walked to the bridge. The soldier stopped his work. A light of recognition touched his eyes. He removed his hat and held it in his hand.

"*Buenos días, señorita,*" he said in a kind voice.

"*Señor,* I am looking for the body of the sergeant you so kindly saved from bitter pain," I said. "Maybe you saw where he was buried."

The soldier nodded. "*Sí,* I know. Follow me."

Catalina and I followed the soldier to the *camposanto,* where bloodstained mule carts were lined up. We worked our way along the gruesome path to a freshly dug trench at the edge of the cemetery. It was piled high with bodies tumbled on top of one another in grotesque positions, so that the hand of one man might be covering the face of another, or the foot of one resting on the belly of another. The older soldier stopped.

"He is down there. I took him out of the wagon myself. I said a prayer over his body and placed him at the far end. You can rest assured the good sergeant was not tossed in like an old rag."

Tears streamed down Catalina's face.

"Muchas gracias, señor," she whispered. She sighed, then drew a handkerchief from her blouse and wiped her eyes. "Poor, poor Sergeant Ildefonso. He was a good man."

"Muchas gracias, señor," I said to the soldier. "It was kind of you to help." I turned to Catalina. "Now I must find Esteban. I know in my heart that he is still alive. I will search the houses where the wounded are kept."

"I will go find your aunt and tell her where the sergeant is buried. Maybe she will get a little peace from knowing his final resting place."

≡ ≡ ≡

After we parted I followed the stream of carts and wagons carrying wounded men to houses in town. Those who could walk were left to fend for themselves; those who were unconscious or prostrate were carried into the houses and stretched on the floors with no mats, no blankets, no pillows.

Inside the first house, I was greeted by the most awful moans of anguish and the sickening stench of fresh and drying blood. The floor was alive with writhing men, their hands covered with blood as they clasped their wounds. No one had cleaned the wounds, for no one had a clean bandage. Some women had torn the men's shirts off and used them to wrap the wounds, but the filthy shirts would probably do more harm than good. There was no gauze. There were no surgeons to remove shrapnel or amputate shattered limbs, no instruments to perform the surgery.

One man with a bloody leg, shattered at the knee, was screaming as his comrade used his hatchet to hack the limb off. The man pleaded for death, then mercifully passed out from the pain. Many lay in quiet agony, waiting for death, calling for their wives or mothers, fathers or comrades. I quickly searched the faces, pale and gray. Esteban was not there.

I left the first house, shaking so badly I was hardly able to stand upright. The second house was even worse. I saw three men who had just died being pulled out so that three more wounded could take their places. It was the same with each house, and my heart sank as each search ended.

Suddenly I saw Aunt Florencia going into a small stucco house removed from the main road. She carried her basket of herbs and medicines and a bundle of rags. I walked as fast as my weak legs would carry me and rushed through the opened door. My aunt was stooped over a man, washing his wounds and tying them with the cloth. Closer now, I saw that the rags were made of strips of colored cloth from women's petticoats.

She glanced up. "I saw Esteban in the next room," she said, as she wrapped a bloody leg. "I'll tend to him as soon as I finish here."

"Esteban!" I shouted, as I rushed into the next room. "Esteban!"

A tiny noise, almost a squeak, came from a soldier propped up against the wall. He was trying to shout, but his breath was shallow and labored. I dropped to my knees and clasped Esteban's hands. They were shaking.

"I am glad to see your ugly brown face, *mi amigo*," Esteban said between painful gasps.

"How bad are you hurt?" I asked, staring at the bloody shirt.

Esteban forced a smile. "It is not so bad. A piece of shrapnel hit me in the chest. It missed my heart, but it hurts a lot when I breathe. There was not much bleeding."

He gritted his teeth, and tears of pain slid from under his thick eyelashes as he settled back down. I removed my coatee and rolled it up to make a pillow.

"My aunt is here. She will tend your wounds," I said. "Are you hungry?"

"No. I have no appetite, but I am so thirsty."

"I will go fetch you some water," I said, and left the room. I found an empty bucket and began searching for a well. There was one in a lovely shaded plaza, surrounded by men and women waiting to get water for their loved ones or the wounded.

Soon after I gave water to Esteban, Aunt Florencia arrived. She washed and dressed the wound as best she could.

"Is the shrapnel still there?" I asked her.

"Oh, yes," she said, with bitterness in her voice. "All the wounded still have lead in them, or a nail, or a piece of horseshoe. There are no tools to remove it. General Santa Anna was more concerned with ammunition and guns than with his soldiers." Her face was set, dark from soot, and her dress was covered with bloodstains. "I have seen death all my life, especially in the Revolution. But this is the most senseless, the most brutal." She paused. "Curses upon Santa Anna. I have run out of rags."

As she spoke, a young captain visiting his men on the other side of the room stepped forward. He removed his sooty, stained blue jacket, then his white cotton shirt. He ripped the shirt into strips and handed them to Aunt Florencia.

"It is the least I can do for the poor wretches," he said softly.

After Aunt Florencia bound Esteban's chest, he fell into a deep sleep. I reluctantly told her that I had found the sergeant's grave and asked if she wanted me to show her. She hesitated a moment, then with a vicious jerk, ripped a piece of cloth in two. "It is too late for the dead," she said in a cold, hard voice. "I must worry about the living."

It was growing dark, and I knew I had to return to the remains of my company. There was no discipline, for each unit still did not know who was wounded, dead, or simply missing. I informed my captain that Esteban was wounded and told him about Sergeant Ildefonso and Lieutenant Ochoa. The captain sank onto a tree stump. He put his face in his hands, then ran his fingers through his tangled hair and stared at the ground. He dismissed me without bothering to look up.

I made my bed on the ground. I thought that I would never sleep again, but to my amazement, I fell into the deep sleep of exhaustion and did not stir until sunrise the next morning. The stench of death smacked me in the face. Though the rebel bodies had been burned, and most of the Mexican soldiers had been buried, some still floated in the river and body parts still lay here and there. Coyotes had come in the night and carried some away. Now buzzards circled overhead.

I visited Esteban every day. Although the wound was not considered a mortal one, he was in too much pain to resume his normal duties and remained in the sick house, on his back. Catalina was relieved to find him still alive and I sometimes saw her in the sick house when she brought him soup and water.

The rest of the Second Division arrived slowly—the artillery on March 8; the second-in-command, General Filisola, on March 9; General Andrade and the cavalry on March 10; and the next day the Tolsa infantry.

As the artillery moved across the plaza, I wondered how many lives would have been spared if General Santa Anna had waited until their arrival. The rebels would have been half starved by then and ready to surrender. Heavy artillery would have been able to breach the walls, letting us avoid the bloody scaling that took so many lives. As each new unit arrived, these were the thoughts of every soldier. Had this battle, this "small affair," been worth the cost? And I could not help but wonder how many more would die by the end of the war.

NINETEEN

A Quiet Death

Morale was low. Even though we had won the battle, the loss was so extreme that most felt it was a fruitless victory. Instead of celebrating with high spirits and a feeling of love for our leader, we felt more like cattle off to the slaughter. Our distrust for His Excellency grew with each day that passed.

Supplies were critically low, our clothing hung in rags, and the wounded suffered unbearable pain for lack of a field hospital. Lead and shrapnel remained in bodies and mutilated limbs were not amputated. Wounds festered and gangrene spread. The less-severely wounded wandered about, their pain making their lives miserable.

And all the while this suffering went on, His Excellency remained oblivious. He visited the houses where the seriously wounded lay stretched on the cold floors and spoke words of encouragement to them. He even told them they would get extra pay. One day after hearing him give this promise to a soldier, I heard His Excellency whisper to his assistant to scratch the man off the list because he would not live to collect.

When the request went out for bandages, all of the officers tore their cotton bed linens into strips. All the officers except one—General Santa Anna. It would appear his fine skin was too delicate to sleep on an uncovered mattress.

Morale was low even among the officers, many of whom had led honorable military careers and were well respected. Many of the unfortunate officers, who had not been paid since the campaign began, were starving.

The sutlers increased their prices to unfathomable degrees. A cartload of corn cost forty-eight *pesos,* almost three months' salary for a private. A cart of beans cost seventy-two *pesos,* and a pound of sugar one *peso*—unobtainable for most. A *piloncillo* of sugar cost four *reales,* and flour was not available at all. Except, of course, to His Excellency. He ate loaves of bread, while his officers and men ate *tortillas* or raw cornmeal. I was not surprised to find out that the provisioner general, the man in charge of the supplies, was His Excellency's own brother-in-law, and was reaping a fortune in profits. For some men, war was a business.

As for tents, His Excellency's was large and fine. The rest of the soldiers slept in small ragged tents, or on the ground, in all kinds of weather. His Excellency had several changes of uniforms and orderlies to wait on him hand and foot. The general's moods were so unpredictable that his officers avoided going into his headquarters at all costs. They said it was the opium that made him act that way, but I thought it was the personality he was born with. All of the possessions of the defeated rebels, including goods from stores in town, were confiscated by His Excellency. After he had selected items for his personal use, the rest were sold at exorbitant prices to soldiers or townspeople.

His Excellency did not express any compassion for the wounded and sick, nor for the dead buried in the cemetery or floating in the river. He never showed remorse for his decision that cost so many brave lives. But he did busy himself with finding a pretty girl to keep him company. Though His Excellency was forty years old, the girl he selected was my age.

Soon a story was circulating that I knew was true. The pretty girl's mother refused to let her stay with the general unless he married her. To appease the mother, His Excellency asked one of his lackey officers to dress in the cloth of a priest and conduct a false marriage ceremony. Perhaps the mother really had no choice, but surely she knew, like everyone else, that the general had a wife and children on his *hacienda* near Jalapa. Nevertheless, the ceremony went forward, and the girl lived with the general throughout his stay in San Antonio de Béxar.

As each day passed, more men died of their wounds. It was almost a relief to see their suffering end. Many fine funerals occurred when officers died, with friends serving as pallbearers, the trumpets playing, and stirring eulogies. When common soldiers died, the lamenting was left to the wives, sisters, children, and fellow soldiers.

Esteban's wound grew worse. It had festered, and the poisonous fluids needed to be drained. It was not the worst of wounds, and if there had been surgeons it could have easily been taken care of. But there were no surgeons. At least Esteban had someone to visit him every day. Most of the wounded suffered and died alone.

On March 11, I heard a commotion and saw a division of soldiers preparing to leave. They included seven hundred infantrymen, one hundred horses, two field cannons with their crews, fifty cases of ammunition, and supply wagons. General Ramírez y Sesma had been ordered to march to San Felipe de Austin, the capital of the Texan colonies, located on the Brazos River, about fifty leagues from San Antonio de Béxar.

Later in the day, yet another division moved out, this time with a twelve-pound cannon, an eight-pounder, a howitzer, and several cases of ammunition. This division took the southern road, marching to Goliad under the command of Colonel Morales, to join General Urrea. General Urrea was the most respected officer in the Texas campaign. He had won every battle he fought in the southern regions of the state, even when he was outnumbered. It was rumored that he always distributed captured goods among his men equally and provided for their needs with local food. And he always made a point of seeking out physicians among the enemy prisoners and using their services. I heard many a soldier wish out loud that it was General Urrea who was leading us, rather than His Excellency.

The sudden activity stirred us out of our stupor. Since the fateful battle at the Alamo on March 6, we had had many days to think of our situation and the miserable lot of our wounded comrades. Most of us were anxious to get on with the campaign.

Rumors flew every day about the enemy; some thought they were regrouping and would attack, others felt the rebels had fled, were disorganized, and in worse condition than we were. We all knew that if the army did not get on the road soon, heavy spring rains would halt the campaign altogether.

On March 15, a messenger from Sesma's division brought word that the Texan town of Gonzales on the Guadalupe River had been abandoned and burned by the enemy. The flames were still streaking the sky as General Sesma and his troops marched into town. They had found some unburnt houses filled with fine possessions and food still on the tables. Outside town, fat cattle roamed the fields, chickens and pigs ran about the yards, cribs were loaded with corn, and the riverbanks were lined with freshly baled cotton of the finest quality.

This news caused a tremendous stir among the soldiers. For the first time since the battle, our spirits lifted. I knew it was only a matter of days until we would move out. And if our enemies were fleeing, taking their families with them, there might not be another battle at all. Nearly every officer felt that the campaign would be over within weeks. This optimism put a song in the heart of every soldier, including mine.

On March 17, even more battalions and artillery left to reinforce Sesma's division on its way northeast to San Felipe and to reinforce General Urrea near Goliad to the south. Instinct told me that my unit would be leaving soon. Part of my heart rejoiced that we would be on the road. The supplies in Béxar had vanished, and we were near starvation and wearing rags. Soon we would be marching where cows roamed free and pigs and chickens ate out of your hand. My mouth watered at the thought of having a full belly for once.

And yet part of me ached with remorse. Esteban had not recuperated from his wound and had gone from bad to worse. He was no longer able to sit up, and half the time his fever caused delirium. Each time I saw him, the pain in his eyes tore into my soul. I did not want to be there, yet I felt it my duty to speak to Esteban, to joke as if nothing were wrong.

On March 19, when I visited the sick house, a local priest and my aunt were at Esteban's side. Esteban gasped for air with each breath, and his voice rattled in his throat as he tried to speak.

When he saw me, his pain-filled eyes glistened with a tiny light.

"Amigo," he said, struggling to speak. "I must tell you something." He lifted his hand and grasped my coat sleeve weakly.

"Shh, do not speak," I whispered, but he did not listen.

"I knew...," He swallowed hard, then coughed up blood. "I knew you were not sixteen. I did remember your father and his broad shoulders. You should not have been conscripted. Your sisters died because of it... Can you forgive me?"

Anger rushed over me, and I felt a heavy lump where my heart should have been. Esteban clung to my coat harder.

"Mi amigo, forgive me," he whispered again.

The priest and Aunt Florencia both looked at me, but I said nothing. My aunt took Esteban's hand as the priest administered last rites and gave him Eucharist. Esteban's face was yellow with death, and a putrid smell rose from his chest. He sipped the Communion wine, choking while swallowing. His eyes began to grow dim as he looked at me.

I thought of my dear little sisters, Señor Sandoval, and the pain my aunt had gone through. All because of Esteban's lie that had put me in the army. Then I looked at the death around me, the suffering. No, it was not Esteban who had caused this great pain. I took Esteban's hand. "I forgive you," I said softly.

Esteban exhaled, his head fell to one side, and his hand went limp. It was a quiet death.

Aunt Florencia did not cry, but expelled a long, weary sigh. We all knew that Esteban was far better off now. As my aunt washed his body and wrapped him in a *sarape* for burial—there was no coffin available in town—I could not help but think about Sergeant Ildefonso's wisdom. He must have witnessed many a soldier linger with mortal wounds. For the first time since the good sergeant's death, I did not feel regret that the stranger had ended his suffering.

■ ■ ■

Over the next few days, we received a series of messages from General Urrea in the southern part of Texas. His forces were defeating the rebels at every turn. First, he defeated them near Goliad and took almost four hundred prisoners, who were now housed in the old *presidio* at La Bahía. Then General Urrea drove his men on a forced march to Guadalupe Victoria and took another one hundred prisoners after a battle. And on the twenty-third, even more prisoners were captured at Cópano, on the Gulf Coast. They were quickly pressed into gangs and forced to rebuild the fort there.

On March 27, my regiment received orders to march. I was relieved to finally be leaving San Antonio de Béxar, for this tragic little town had brought nothing but pain, misery, and heartache to the Mexican army. The smell of death still lingered in the air.

His Excellency reviewed the troops himself on March 28, and again on the twenty-ninth. Excitement and anticipation tingled my spine as I marched in the line, musket on my shoulder, uniform cleaned for the occasion. With us were twenty mounted dragoons, about five hundred infantrymen, the pickets of all the corps combined, one howitzer, fifty crates of ammunition, and food rations.

■ ■ ■

On the afternoon we left, I had decided to pay a quick visit to the grave of Esteban to say a final good-bye. I found Catalina there, placing a bouquet of wildflowers on the mound of earth where Esteban was buried. Seeing her there on her knees, whispering soft prayers and bidding Esteban *adiós*, almost moved me to tears. She had only one goat left, the nanny that had tripped me the day I was conscripted from the fields. Although the goat had barely survived the long journey, she was now growing fat on the spring grasses.

"What will you do?" I asked, as Catalina rose. Her eyes, lined with dark circles, and her emaciated body almost made her look like a stranger. I longed to hear her laughter and see the dimples in her cheeks as she made faces and scoffed at me.

"I have only two choices," she said. "I can stay here and try to survive, or I can follow the army and try to survive."

"Aunt Florencia says she is going to stay here and care for the sick and wounded," I said. "I just said good-bye to her."

Catalina nodded. "Since there are no doctors, she is of great value here. But there are many widows and orphans like me following the army. They think their chances are better there. Maybe I can find a place with them."

"If you decide to follow the army, I will visit you every chance I get. And after this war is over, I will take you and my aunt back to San Javier."

Catalina's eyes widened a moment, then clouded over. "There is nothing waiting for me there, either. I have no more future than a motherless coyote lost in the mountains. Look at me, Lorenzo. I am penniless. I have no family. I have only one goat. Who wants to marry a girl with only one goat?"

I could not help but smile. "Do not worry. I will find a solution. I promise."

She cocked her head to one side and forced a weak smile. "When did you become a man, Lorenzo Bonifacio?"

"When did you become a woman?" I replied.

The bugle sounded muster, and I had to leave Catalina. As soldiers lifted knapsacks to their shoulders and formed lines, their spirits were higher than at any time since the campaign had begun. Inspired by General Urrea's recent victories, we were full of pride and love of country. We wanted our dead comrades to be avenged and knew that it was only a matter of time before the enemy would be defeated and driven from Mexican lands altogether. Mexico would be free of foreign invaders, and we would go home, proud and victorious.

TWENTY

The Advance

Our division pulled out of town around four in the afternoon. As we marched past the ruins of the Alamo, my heart ached. Here we had fought a vain and pointless battle and lost the flower of our army for no cause other than the egotism of His Excellency.

During our stay in Béxar, we received word that the minister of war, safely nestled in Mexico City, had called the Texas campaign an amusement show, with incompetent soldiers and useless officers. His insults aroused the anger and hatred of every common soldier and many of the officers, too. He challenged the loyalty and patriotism of the Mexican soldier, when, in fact, we were the ones suffering starvation and inclement weather and casualties. Yet, the soldiers did not rebel, for it is the nature of Mexican soldiers to suffer grievances without complaint.

The day after we left Béxar, a sudden and violent storm dumped rain on our column, but we continued onward. After the rain stopped, the roads were deep with mud, making it almost impossible for the wagons and carts to travel. The road was called El Camino Real—the King's Highway—for it was the highway first forged by the Spaniards over a hundred years ago between eastern Texas and Mexico City. We took turns pushing the wagons and made poor time.

A strange and beautiful sight greeted our eyes near Cibolo Creek—an immense herd of buffalo. I watched in awe as the herd rumbled by, taking two full hours. It made me think of the *indios* who lived in the region, especially those like the Comanche, who were said to ride horses and were dependent on the buffalo for survival. I admired the woolly creatures, with their immense size and strength, and could easily see why some of the *indios* worshiped them as gods. Our column was helpless to cross the creek until the herd had passed by.

The next day we ran out of water, for in spite of the rain, there were no creeks, only an occasional puddle of mud not fit to drink. The soldiers were miserable. We had not eaten meat since the day before leaving Béxar. We had been told there would be food at the Texan colony of Gonzales on the Guadalupe River. But the rain and mud had delayed our journey. Mercifully, on April 1, we spied some *tejano* ranchers leading a herd of three hundred fine cattle. The ranchers generously gave us three yearlings to slaughter, and we satisfied our hunger.

The following day the rains came again, causing us to get a very late start. We had traveled about three leagues when a messenger arrived saying that His Excellency, General Santa Anna, who had left Béxar two days after us, was not far behind. His Excellency ordered that our column stop the march and wait for him. I heard several officers grumble over the absurdity of this order.

"He acts more like a king than a general," one officer said. "It is unheard of to stop a march for the sake of a general."

"He probably lagged behind to have a final night of passion with his child bride," a soldier shouted, causing a great roar of laughter to ripple down the line.

General Santa Anna arrived with much fanfare. I wonder how many of the soldiers were cursing him under their breath, like me. The march resumed, passing through some of the most beautiful country ever beheld by the eyes of man. Spring had arrived. As we climbed gently rolling hills, the wildflowers spread out in front of us like blankets of blue, orange, yellow, purple, white, and palest pink. The fragrance wafted in the air, and birds of every kind sang joyous songs in greeting. How different this land was from the rugged, uninhabited part of Texas I had first seen. This was a paradise, and now I easily understood why the Texans were bent on having it for themselves.

As the column approached the Guadalupe River, we entered a pleasant woods that hugged the banks, creating a haven for birds and other wildlife. The river itself had steep, rocky banks, and the water ran clear and very cold. The recent rains had swollen the river, making it too high for the wagons and carts to ford, so we were ordered to camp until the waters subsided. Every soldier was happy to pitch camp in such a Garden of Eden.

But our peace was short-lived. It was April 2, the day before Easter, that most holy of days, that we received disturbing news. We learned that the four hundred *norteamericano* prisoners at Goliad had been mercilessly massacred on March 27, Palm Sunday. The rebels had surrendered in hopes of being given amnesty. General Urrea, who had captured them, was not present, having gone on to the next battle, but he had left instructions for the prisoners to be spared and used as forced labor. But General Santa Anna gave orders for their execution, claiming that his policy of no quarter must be followed as an example for the colonists and insurgents.

"The helpless prisoners were unarmed," said the messenger who brought the news, "and told they were being taken out of the *presidio* to be released. They broke into song as they marched along, happy at the thought of rejoining their friends and loved ones. They were taken out in three groups and marched in different directions. The latter groups heard shots and came to realize that their comrades had been killed, and knew that they would be next. The wounded, left in the *presidio* infirmary, also heard the shots and knew what was in store for them. Their injured leader, Colonel Fannin, was executed as he sat in a chair."

A clamor of disgust rose among the soldiers at this news. Though we had killed the rebels at the Alamo, the enemy there had fought bravely. No one believed that executing unarmed prisoners was an honorable thing, even in times of war. Men imprisoned and out of the way were of no harm. And that General Urrea had urged they be spared made us all the more furious.

On Easter, His Excellency crossed the Guadalupe River and continued his journey to San Felipe. He left his second-in-command, General Filisola, in charge. Perhaps His Excellency did not want to be around his disgruntled men. If they had not respected him before, now they came close to loathing him altogether. I was more than happy to see the general and his lackeys disappear from the camp.

That same morning we said prayers among ourselves, since there was no priest for mass. Every man's thoughts turned to home and those loved ones who had accompanied him to mass in times past. I searched for Catalina among the women and children. I saw her talking and strolling with a soldier. Jealousy singed me like a hot cinder. I wanted to follow them, but my captain was waving me over to help with the building of a barge.

My strong back and swimming skills were very useful during the eastward advance. Streams and rivers were swollen from uncommonly heavy spring rains and had to be sounded. I enjoyed being a swimmer—the cool water on a hot day, the feeling of floating. But it was very dangerous work.

The captain handed me the end of a long rope, and I swam across the swiftly moving river. Twice the strong current grabbed me and would have pulled me downstream were it not for two fellow soldiers holding the rope.

On the third try, I made it across and secured the rope to a cypress tree. I recrossed the river, this time with the aid of the rope to keep me afloat. I carried a second rope across and secured it, also. Painstakingly, we built a barge out of logs and ropes. Using poles and the ropes as guides, we slowly began transporting men, wagons, animals, and supplies across.

The Guadalajara Battalion began crossing at midday, and the supplies came across little by little. Night fell before all the men and supplies had been ferried, so some camped in Gonzales, others on the opposite bank. After dark I crept to the women's camp and tried to find Catalina, but no one had seen her since that morning. I spent a restless night thinking about her and the soldier.

The next morning dawned clear and cool, with the eastern sky streaked with gold and pink. The remainder of the soldiers and supplies crossed the river, and for a little while I had the opportunity to explore Gonzales. It lay in ruins; nearly all of the houses had been burned earlier by the settlers as they fled eastward. But the shells of some of the houses remained, and here and there outside the town, a house had survived intact. Most of the dwellings were constructed of logs and consisted of one room and a stone chimney, or two rooms with an open breezeway between each room. As usual, General Ramírez y Sesma and his army of women followers had passed through days before and taken everything of value they could carry with them.

Some pigs rooted in yards, fat cattle grazed in the fields, and family dogs and cats wandered around with forlorn expressions. Cotton, much of it already ginned and baled, lined the riverbanks, waiting to be carried to the Gulf of Mexico. There were many items I had never seen before and could not fathom what they had been used for. But some were very ingenious—a machine for removing hard corn from its cob, another for grinding the corn into meal, as well as spinning wheels, looms, and sundry quaint and mysterious household items. The furniture, mostly constructed from local wood, was sturdy and functional.

The sight of so much industry and so many products of years of hard labor amazed me. It must have been hard for them to leave their prized possessions. Seeing children's toys and clothing and baby's cradles especially bothered me; I couldn't help but think that these children were now suffering from rain and mud and disease like us, as they fled east. The Mexican soldiers had been told again and again that the *norteamericanos* were cruel barbarians, who cared neither for their children nor for God. But I saw many graves with crosses, causing me to doubt everything I had heard.

I began to feel sorry for the settlers who had come to Texas legally and who had peacefully tilled the soil and wanted nothing but to raise their families and be left alone. How many of those settlers actually took part in the revolt? I wondered. How many of their men had joined the cause, not thinking ahead about what pain it might cause their women and children? How many little innocent babies would die in the arms of their mothers because of the foolishness of some land-greedy foreigners who had interfered with the affairs of the settlers and caused this war to descend upon them?

The officers told us we could forage for chickens, eggs, and pigs. Sometimes the sight was comical. But the cattle were off-limits to all the soldiers. A party of Sesma's men had stayed behind. The colonel left in charge of them had gathered a herd of one thousand cattle and allowed no one to touch them. He planned to start a colony of Mexican soldiers and their families after the war, and the livestock would be divided among them. He also confiscated shanks of cured ham from the settlers' smokehouses and corn from the cribs. So, in spite of plentiful beef, the common soldiers received only small rations.

On April 5, I received pay for my work building the barge. General Filisola paid the workers and swimmers out of his own pocket. Though he was Italian, rather than Mexican, and was often criticized by officers for his indecision, I found him to be a gentle person, who only reluctantly accepted his position of second-in-command. He seemed to know instinctively that whenever anything went wrong, His Excellency would blame him, and whenever anything went right, His Excellency would take all the credit.

More men and artillery arrived, and on April 6, we resumed the eastward march. We came across many farms that had escaped being burned, for they were far removed from the town. Corral fences were built of the most unique patterns, not made of *adobe* or stone but lengths of cut timbers placed at angles. The captain called it "sawtooth" fashion, for indeed the fences viewed from a distance gave the appearance of the teeth of a saw.

Our brigade fell into a set routine, waking at reveille, breaking camp, and leaving by eight o'clock each day. We marched through fields of breathtaking beauty, crossed creeks, traversed woods, and camped near water when possible. A certain boredom soon set in, for most felt that the war was over and that we were marching for no reason. The enemy had fled, leaving his possessions, his crops, his livestock behind. He had burned most of his houses and appeared to have left Texas altogether. Perhaps because of this tedium some of the soldiers and women began vandalizing the houses they found, ripping apart clothing and fine furniture for the sport of it. Card games flourished nightly, and also cockfights— anything to relieve the monotony.

One day I found a small gold locket whose chain had broken. With a little work I was able to repair it. It would make a pretty gift for Catalina, if I could find her. She had been avoiding me, there was no doubt in my mind. Each time I sought her out, either early in the morning or in the evening after camp had been pitched, she was nowhere to be found. I could not even determine which group of women she was traveling with.

On April 9, we reached Navidad Creek. Many of the wagons could not cross, so they were left behind and the army continued the march. With luck, the wagons would catch up by that night. We received word that His Excellency had arrived at San Felipe, the capital of the Texas colonists. He found that the town had been burned and the enemy had retreated.

The rains continued to fall often. The road was intolerable in places, full of deep mud and holes that broke axles. It was slow going, but on the tenth, at last we came to the Colorado River. The river was large and swollen from the rains.

There I saw African slaves. They had either been abandoned or had escaped in the confusion of the colonists' retreat. There was a mulatto woman, two *negro* women, and several *negro* men. They greeted our troops as liberators, for the Mexican government forbids slavery. The general declared them to be free citizens of Mexico. The Negroes were very eager to help. The men, who were well-built and strong, helped with the crossing, and the women washed the officers' clothes.

The crossing of the river took three days. On one of those days, two *anglo* boys wandered into the camp. They explained, through an interpreter, that they had been out hunting for two days, and when they returned home their cabin was abandoned, and all the neighbors were gone, too. They had been feeding themselves but were scared and did not know what was happening.

They were polite, well-behaved boys, one with yellow hair, the other with red hair and freckles. Their blue eyes reminded me of the youth at the Alamo who had stared at me before dying. I wondered if these two had kin killed in that fateful battle.

Two officers quickly offered to adopt the boys, for children are well loved in my culture. But a French trapper and his wife, who had not taken sides in this war, agreed to take care of the boys.

By the evening of April 13, the last of the wagons had crossed the Colorado River. The officers decided to leave the cattle behind because the herd could not maneuver the steep banks and swift current. That same day we received word that General Ramírez y Sesma had crossed the Brazos several leagues ahead of us to the east. The bugler quickly sounded reveille and several salvos were shot into the air. It was not such a grand thing to celebrate, but we were desperate for something to do, other than walk through mud and cross rivers.

We began the march again on April 14. We marched across an immense plain until we were almost at the Brazos River. In the distance we saw strange forms sticking in the air. They turned out to be the chimneys of the burnt-out cabins at San Felipe de Austin.

The town was situated on a gentle slope that rolled down to the river. There were many wells, each one deep and lined with brick. The buckets were made of wood and perfectly round. The men took turns drinking with a gourd dipper. Never had I tasted water so cool and sweet. I could easily imagine the peace and prosperity of this town before it was abandoned.

Two stores filled with food and supplies had been destroyed, and the soldiers picked over the ruins looking for anything of value. I found a coffee grinder and a bag of pecans. I traded them for a new pair of sandals and a piece of sweet cake that one of the women had made. I splurged because I was celebrating the day of my birth sixteen years ago. I did not feel sixteen. Instead, I felt like an old man.

The generals decided not to cross the Brazos here but to turn south. It was rumored that the Texan army under the command of General Sam Houston had already crossed and was someplace in hiding along the opposite banks.

On April 15, about seven in the morning, a great commotion arose. I heard shots and every man ran for his musket, sure that the enemy was commencing a surprise attack. I ran to the river just in time to see a strange contraption churning downstream. It was a boat like none I had ever seen, with huge puffs of smoke chugging from metal pipes. *Norteamericanos* were on the boat shouting at us. The bright red-white-and-blue flag of the United States waved in the wind on its prow.

The Mexican soldiers shouted back at the *Gautdam-yees,* as we now called them, for those were the main words we heard from them during the battle at the Alamo. We fired muskets and the eight-pound cannon at them, but all our lead fell in the river, for the boat was running too fast and was going with the current. The captain told us it was called a "steamboat," and that it was driven by coal or wood fires that created steam and drove motors. We talked about it for hours.

After the excitement, I decided to explore a house with a pretty peach orchard, its trees covered in soft pink blossoms. I saw a girl stooped in a garden, digging potatoes with a butcher knife and dropping them into her cupped *rebozo.* When she turned her head slightly, I was shocked to see that it was Catalina. I ran to her and dropped to my knees. She slowly turned her head.

"Catalina!" I gasped. "What happened to you?" Her face was bruised and swollen, one eye closed almost shut. She let the potatoes drop and lifted her *rebozo* to cover her face.

"Do not look at me," she sobbed. "I am hideous." Her shoulders shook. I gently pulled the cloth down and lifted her chin.

"Who did this to you?"

She shook her head. "I do not know his name. A soldier."

"Did he violate you?"

She hesitated a moment. "No. He tried, but I got away."

"I will kill him. You have to point him out to me." My voice shook with rage. My heart pounded furiously.

Catalina looked at the ground. "I—I did not see him clearly. It was dark. Please, do not be angry."

I felt a knot twisting in my stomach and my throat grew tight. I had never felt more helpless. I wanted to scream, but held my breath instead until I could not stand it another moment.

"Where have you been, Catalina? I have been searching for you for days."

Her face slowly turned upward again. Two streams of tears flowed down her grimy cheeks. "I was so ashamed. I didn't want you to see me like this." She paused. "Look, I found some *patatas*. I will be all right." She began picking the potatoes up and dropping them back into her cupped *rebozo*. I methodically helped her until it was full.

"Shall I walk beside you?" I asked, when she finally rose.

"You are so sweet to worry about me. But I will be all right. I was careless. It will not happen again." She held up the butcher knife she was using to dig potatoes. "I found this over there," she said, nodding toward a half-burnt cabin. "I'm not afraid to use it."

The bugler sounded the call to march. We looked in the direction of the slowly moving army. "I have a gift for you," I said, and gave her the locket I had found earlier.

"Oh, Lorenzo, it is so beautiful. I will wear it forever." She clasped it around her neck. Even her pleasant smile could not bring beauty to her tortured face this time.

"I will visit you tonight," I said. "Where will you be?"

Catalina glanced at the company of women spilling onto the road behind the troops. "I will be all right, Lorenzo. I promise you. I'll find you this evening and we'll talk. I have not forgotten that yesterday was your birthday. You are sixteen at last." She placed her cool fingers against my cheek, then turned and ran. I watched her vanish into the group of women before trotting to catch up with my regiment.

I could think of nothing else but Catalina as I walked along. I examined the face of every man around me, wondering, *Is he the one? Is he the man who beat Catalina and tried to deflower her?* Maybe she was not telling the truth; maybe he had succeeded. Her face would heal and return to its former charm, but what about her soul?

Her spirit seemed to be subdued, defeated. For that, I could never forgive the monster that harmed her.

■ ■ ■

During afternoon *siesta* I searched for Catalina, but once again she had vanished. I did not know which of the women were her friends, if any. Those I asked said they did not know her, and the ones who seemed to know her merely shrugged and said they were not responsible for her whereabouts. Some of them were prostitutes, unsavory women who followed the army, selling their bodies in exchange for money, food, or anything of value the soldiers possessed.

At the end of the day, we had traveled over seven leagues, a decent distance considering the condition of the road. We camped that night at a burnt-out farm. I waited most of the night for Catalina to find me, but she did not come. My heart was so heavy I could not breathe well, and when I awoke I was as tired as when I had gone to bed.

April 16 brought another severe storm. The roads and ground, still deep with mud from previous rains, now were more impassable than ever. We traveled less than five leagues the whole day, and I was too busy helping push wagons from the mud to think of anything else. We reached a locale on the Brazos River called Thompson's Pass. Why it was called a pass, I did not know, for the red, sandy banks of the river here were thirty feet steep. There was no barge and no boatman. And the Brazos was the widest and swiftest of all the rivers we had crossed so far. The arduous task of getting men, artillery, wagons, and mules across the river took two full days.

On April 18, a courier arrived with urgent orders from General Santa Anna, causing excitement to rustle through the encampment. General Cós was ordered to take five hundred men on a forced march and join Santa Anna and the vanguard army, now located near a small settlement called Harrisburg. General Houston had been found, and Santa Anna was determined to destroy the Texan army once and for all. His Excellency also sent instructions that the women and children were not to come along; they were to stay at Thompson's Pass, for their presence would slow the march too much.

My company was one of the chosen, along with the remnants of the Aldama and Toluca, two companies from Guadalajara, and the Guerrero Battalion. Excitement consumed me at the prospects of another battle. Boredom had made me forget the bloody scene from six weeks ago. My only regret was not seeing Catalina. There was no way of knowing how much longer this campaign might last, or if I would see her again, should it end. Suddenly I knew I had to find Catalina and say good-bye, possibly for the last time.

TWENTY-ONE
■ ■ ■ ■ ■ ■ ■ ■ ■ ■

Toward Destiny

General Cós allowed us a few moments to say fare-well to our families. All around, I heard women weeping and wailing. They had traveled through the worst hardships imaginable, endured starvation, thirst, disease, and death alongside their men. Some were heavy with child. Some had given birth along the way and now carried infants on their backs or slung around their stomachs in their *rebozos*. They had suffered even more than the common soldier. Their once-great number of about fifteen hundred was now reduced to less than five hundred. They suffered greatly carrying part of their loved ones' heavy gear. Of one thing I was sure: No other soldier in the history of warfare ever carried more use-less tools and baggage than the Mexican soldier. We had neither corn to eat nor water to drink, but by *Dios*, we had shovels to dig graves for our dead.

I searched for Catalina, and had almost given up finding her when I heard her voice and saw the familiar long braid and bright skirt. Catalina was standing next to an officer, and he was pressing something into her hand.

"Catalina!" I shouted, my voice cracking with anger.

The soldier glanced my way, then replaced his hat. He placed a rough kiss on Catalina's lips. "I will see you soon," he said, then spun on his heels and trotted away to join his company, one that had not been ordered to move out.

"Who was that soldier?" I asked, as I caught up with Catalina. Her face was pale and tears spilled from her eyes.

"He is no one," she whispered.

"Is he the man who beat you?" I clenched my fists, trying to control my anger.

She looked at the ground. *"Sí."*

"Why were you talking to him? What was he giving you?"

She slowly opened her fist. Two small silver coins twinkled in the sunlight. "This is why I am with him," she replied in a raspy voice. "He has given me silver for the pleasure of my company. He promises not to beat me again."

I felt heat flooding my face. "You sold your body for pieces of silver?"

Catalina stepped forward, her slender brown fingers

reaching out toward me. I stepped back in horror, as if she were a monster.

"No, not yet. But don't you understand, Lorenzo? Without a family, a woman cannot survive. That officer has promised me more silver if I will go to him tonight."

"What about your goats? I thought they were your wealth."

"My last goat was stolen and slaughtered a week ago. I have nothing. Nothing."

"You are wrong, Catalina. You have your self-respect and your dignity. If you go to that officer, then you truly will have nothing. You should have come to me for help; I would have shared my rations. I can help you find more goats. You did not have to resort to this. What would your grandfather say? How could you even think of dishonoring the Sandoval name?"

Tears welled in her eyes just as the bugle sounded.

"Lorenzo, do not judge me so harshly. Your friendship is so precious to me, don't you know that? I am here because of you. If you forsake me, then I have no reason to live." She stepped closer, and her cool fingertips managed to touch my cheek. My heart thundered.

"I have to go now," I said.

She held her hand out. "Take this silver. You may need it for supplies along the way."

I recoiled as if she held out a serpent. "I would rather starve than touch that money."

"I will pray for you," she said softly. "Will you pray for me?"

I glared at her shimmering eyes and her softly quivering lips. I urged the words to rise to my tongue, to tell her that I would always love her no matter what she did. But I could not speak.

Catalina nodded. "I understand. And I do not blame you. God be with you, Lorenzo Bonifacio."

She turned and ran toward the women's camp, her legs flying through the field of wildflowers.

I wanted to run after her and tell her I was sorry, but a fellow soldier grabbed my arm. "Hurry, *compadre,* General Cós is impatient."

■ ■ ■

I joined my unit and we crossed the raging river with much difficulty. We were ordered to leave all unnecessary baggage behind and carry only our muskets and cartridge belts. The captain shouted, "Forward, march!" and the column surged forward as if *el diablo* was on its heels.

We stopped for nothing. We did not eat; we did not drink, except from small pools of muddy water along the way. The heat of the day rose and our tongues hung from our mouths like those of exhausted dogs.

We marched like this until darkness swallowed us up. Through the ignorance of a tracker, we got lost in the woods and stumbled about like chickens in a rainstorm. It was only after some of the men began to collapse from exhaustion that we were ordered to stop. There was no time to pitch camp or cook food. Besides, we were too tired to eat. We slumped to the cold, damp ground and slept like dead men. I did not care, for the exhaustion kept me from thinking of Catalina.

Before dawn we dragged our sore bodies up from the ground and started again. We still did not eat. The general said there would be food at Harrisburg, so the sooner we got there, the sooner we would eat and rest. It was a poor incentive, but the only one we had.

Early in the morning, a courier rode past on his way from Santa Anna to the troops still camped at the Brazos River. We rested while the messenger told General Cós that Harrisburg had been burned on orders of Santa Anna. The courier said that His Excellency himself lit a torch and helped start the fire. The false government, who so audaciously had declared Texas a free republic on March 2, had been moving from one settlement to the next, and had left Harrisburg only hours before His Excellency arrived. As the courier described El Presidente's annoyance at having just missed his enemy's leaders, I was very glad I had not been near His Excellency at that moment.

As we plodded along, I could not help but think about the pitiful state of the Mexican army. Our uniforms were in rags, torn, filthy, and mismatched. Most men had long ago lost their shirts, which had either rotted off or been given to comrades to wrap wounds. The uniform coats, being made of wool, chafed the skin, causing rashes, bumps, and oozing sores. Our trousers were in little better condition, and our shoes were either nonexistent or worn with so many holes that we might as well have been barefoot. Some of the Indian conscripts had made new sandals from materials they found in the desert along the way, but most of the men had only the hardened soles of their feet to tread upon.

During the march, an occasional soldier complained of his plight loud enough that the captain, or sergeant, or whoever happened to be closest, clearly heard. Sometimes the complaints were biting, yet so truthful and funny that the rest of the column and even the officers could not help but laugh.

The terrain grew flatter and lower. We saw swamps where frightening-looking alligators sank into muddy waters leaving only their large yellow eyes visible. On April 20, we heard distant noises that sounded like cannons. It struck a sense of urgency in General Cós, and we plunged onward, hardly stopping for more than an hour or two during the night for rest.

On April 21, we at last arrived at the plain where the tents of General Santa Anna's vanguard forces were pitched. It was a low-lying area, with a bayou and stretch of tall grasses to the front, a woods and river to the right, woods and a lake to the rear, and an open plain to the left flank.

The Mexican troops in the distance saw us approaching and a little shout rose from the ranks. I glanced at my fellow comrades. If it was strong enforcements they were expecting, I was afraid they would be disappointed. I was pleased to see Hector, from my village, walking across the field.

"What, you have not been eaten by the buzzards yet?" Hector said, grinning.

"I am too skinny and tough for even a buzzard," I replied, as I removed my musket and collapsed to the ground. "Are the *norteamericanos* nearby? We thought we heard cannonade yesterday."

Hector nodded. "*Sí*, they are here. On the other side of that little rise of tall grass to the front. They have their backs to Buffalo Bayou, a foolish tactic for they will have no place to escape. They have two cannons to our one. Yesterday we had a small skirmish, but they refused to come out and engage us in battle. A mistake on the part of their leader, General Houston. Yesterday they outnumbered us clearly; today we have five hundred more men."

I snorted and glanced at my comrades who had been in the forced march. They breathed heavily, sweat streaming down their faces, their limbs shaking from fatigue.

"If the enemy attacked us this moment, I would be too tired to lift a finger in my defense."

Hector laughed. "A little food and a good sleep will make you as good as new. We are exhausted, too. We stayed up the whole night long digging trenches and piling breastworks in preparation for a dawn attack. But when the sun rose, General Houston did not attack. We waited and waited. Now we are suspicious that he has crossed the river and retreated, as he has been doing since early March. General Santa Anna says we will drive Houston and the rebels to the Sabine River and plant our eagle in the banks."

"Well, I, for one, hope Señor Houston retreats all the way to the United States and leaves us alone," I mumbled.

Hector put his arm around my shoulder and led me toward the camp. "Come eat a meal with me. It is almost *siesta* time. All of us are exhausted and looking forward to some sleep."

As we walked across the plain, I saw the silken tent of His Excellency, its flaps softly rustling in the wind. I thought I saw a young woman inside but could not be sure. It would not surprise me. His Excellency was standing outside the tent engaged in a heated discussion with his brother-in-law General Cós.

I sat beside Hector and ate voraciously. Though the rations were skimpy, never had cold beef and beans tasted so good. That afternoon we received word that we would be allowed to take our *siesta* as usual. El Presidente was confident that Houston would not attack after having seen the arrival of reinforcements. I bade farewell to Hector and returned to my unit.

We stacked our muskets and found places to curl up in the grass. I rolled up my *sarape* for a pillow. The warm sun and soft breeze felt luscious. A sense of relief moved over my body. The enemy was probably across the Sabine River by now. The war was surely over. A deep sleep overcame me, the sweetest sleep I had known in days.

I was dreaming of Catalina skipping through a field of wildflowers, gathering bouquets, and weaving them around the necks of her beloved goats. She smiled and beckoned with her arms, tossing her long shiny hair. I ran after her, laughing, feeling as free as a bird. I must have smiled in my sleep, so pleasant was the dream. Catalina waited for me beside the river, and to my surprise dear Sergeant Ildefonso, Esteban, old Señor Sandoval, and my precious sisters were waiting for me, too. They hugged Catalina as she gave them each a bouquet. I ran as fast as I could, and all turned toward me, smiling warmly.

Suddenly I stumbled on a big rock. I felt myself tumbling, tumbling toward the river. Its water changed from gentle ripples to a raging torrent, slapping against the rocks. I heard Catalina shriek and looked up to see her face contorted with fear and worry. Then I heard Sergeant Ildefonso yelling, *"Get up, Lorenzo!"* and I heard Esteban shouting, *"Look out, Lorenzo!"* My foot got tangled and I fell and fell and fell.

I awoke with a start. I heard a drum and fife playing a lively tune from the direction of the tall grass to the front. Suddenly a cannon boomed, spraying the sleeping soldiers with metal. Men screamed and jumped to their feet.

"To arms! To arms!" my captain shouted. *"Norteamericanos* are attacking!"

TWENTY-TWO

San Jacinto

I leaped up to run for my gun, but another blast from the enemy cannon exploded into the stack of muskets, shattering them to pieces. The enemy was everywhere—on horseback, on foot, coming over the rise, popping up out of the tall grass in front, cutting off escape to the open field on the left. All around the camp, Texans appeared, screaming bloodcurdling cries, shooting with deadly accuracy, and slashing with their sabers.

In the confusion and smoke, I could not find a musket. None of my company could. I heard General Castrillón shouting orders on one side and Colonel Almonte shouting orders on the other. One commander cried out, "Commence firing," and another shouted, "Get down for cover."

I saw a loaded pistol on the ground and picked it up, determined to at least die fighting. A giant *norte-americano* on a buckskin horse thundered across the plain

255

toward me, screaming at the top of his lungs. I did not understand the language, but I recognized the words *Alamo* and *Goliad*. I did not need to speak English to realize that it was revenge for his fallen comrades that the rebel sought. I aimed the pistol and pulled the trigger.

Nothing happened. The powder was too damp to fire.

I threw the useless gun down and ran toward the woods. The Texan was gaining ground, almost at me, when a Mexican soldier jumped at the charging horse with his bayonet, screaming "*¡Viva México!*" at the top of his lungs. The rebel swung his saber at the poor soldier's neck, cutting his head half off. An evil river of red spurted onto the green grass.

A crew of Mexican soldiers got to our only cannon, a nine-pounder nicknamed *El Volcán,* and filled it with grapeshot and balls, bravely firing it again and again. Other soldiers formed ranks at the earthen breastworks and fired volleys at the Texans. But in only a few moments, the Texans' twin cannons smashed the breastworks and the rebels streamed into the camp.

I watched in terror as the enemy overran our camp, massacring my unarmed comrades who had not been able to get to their weapons or horses. Seeing the futility of the situation, our officers ordered retreat. In total confusion and still unarmed, our soldiers ran any way they could to escape the incensed Texans. I managed to scramble up a tall oak tree unnoticed.

The Texans were everywhere at once, chasing us down, blocking those who fled. I saw Mexican soldiers run for the swampy lake. They dived into the waters, some flailing their arms and screaming because they did not know how to swim. Others collided into each other and formed a jam. The Texans calmly and methodically fired into the water, killing them like fish in a shallow pond, until the water ran red with their blood.

I watched General Castrillón, the dear old soldier who had tried in vain to save the lives of the seven rebels who had surrendered at the Alamo, standing on a wagon. With sword in hand he fought off the enemy as bravely as any man could, shouting, "I've never run from a battle yet, and I'm too old to start now." He, too, was killed and fell limp to the ground.

All around me I saw acts of cruelty as my unarmed comrades tried in vain to surrender and begged for mercy. Some of them were near my own age, but they, too, were mowed down with gunfire and sabers. Some of my comrades called out in what little English they knew: "Me no Alamo! Me no Goliad!" but their cries fell on deaf ears. Some threw up their hands in the sign of surrender or dropped to their knees and clasped the legs of the rebels and begged eloquently for mercy in our native Spanish, saying they had wives and children, swearing they had not taken part at Goliad or the Alamo. But all in vain; the enemy had no mercy to give this day.

I saw an exceptionally tall *norteamericano* wearing a broad-brimmed hat and riding a white horse. He seemed to be the commander, and I guessed him to be General Sam Houston. His beautiful white horse was shot out from under him, and he quickly found another and mounted it. This animal, too, was shot out from under him, and he found a third. His foot dripped blood as he rode about. At the sight of his men killing unarmed soldiers, he tried to stop the carnage, but it was too late. The taste of revenge was too sweet. The incensed rebels ignored the orders of their shouting officers.

During the heat of the battle, I saw His Excellency, Santa Anna, pacing in front of his tent, wringing his hands wildly, unable to take command. The next time I looked in that direction El Presidente was gone.

A few of the Mexican soldiers managed to get across the river and vanish into the woods; many climbed trees like me or hid in the tall grass. I saw no opportunity to run. I clung to the tree, shaking and praying that I would not be discovered. After a few moments, the battle was over. Amazingly, the sun had hardly moved; the battle lasted less than half an hour.

The Texans rousted soldiers from their hiding places the rest of the afternoon until it turned dark. Soon the sound of frogs and crickets mingled with the ring of an occasional musket or the *avemarías* of the dying left on the field. Prisoners were rounded up and herded into a circle. I saw several familiar faces and was thankful they had been spared, but if the rebels decided to treat them like the prisoners at Goliad, I knew the captured men were doomed.

That night the rebels built a tremendous fire in the woods. Its flame rose into the sky like an orange monster, consuming entire trees, which had been felled to feed its blaze. The prisoners were herded around it and watched over by dozens of enemy. Each Texan was armed as if for Armageddon. They had five or six guns each and large cloth pouches filled with ammunition. They held candles in their hands and watched over the prisoners vigilantly. The sight of the fire reminded me of the funeral pyre on which the Alamo defenders had been tossed. I expected to see the prisoners thrown into the flames at any moment as an act of retaliation.

With such thoughts as these, I remained in the tree all night. In the morning light the most horrific sight greeted my eyes. The field was strewn with hundreds of my fallen comrades, their corpses and the earth now covered with black blood. The mortally wounded had been left there with no assistance, and they writhed in pain. Overhead, buzzards circled, preparing for their grisly feast.

My heart ached as I stared at the still forms of men whom only yesterday I had dined and drunk with, whom I had joked with and complained to about my throbbing feet. It looked like six hundred Mexicans lay there on the dirt, while the rebels had hardly lost a man.

A sickening feeling overcame me and with it a hatred for El Presidente, who had caused this humiliating situation.

The Texans brought in stragglers all day, found hiding in trees or in the bayou or the tall grass. As one Texan boy brought in a prisoner, whispers rippled among the captured men. Though the new prisoner was wearing the clothes of a private, he had the white skin of an upper-class *criollo*.

The sight of His Excellency disguised as a private made me shudder with hatred and disgust. The general had not stood and fought; he had not even surrendered with honor. He had run like a coward. It was apparent that the boy in charge of this prisoner had no idea whom he had captured. Suddenly, I could not hold in my hatred another moment.

"El Presidente!" I shouted at the top of my lungs, running the risk of revealing my hiding place.

Soon other soldiers, simple privates who had been dragged from their cornfields, who had marched hundreds of miles across deserts and suffered starvation and thirst, who had lost wives and children in blizzards and raging rivers, shouted, "El Presidente!"

The rebels reacted just as I hoped they would. They looked at the man and, as if for the first time noticing his silk shirt and diamond studs, rushed upon him and pointed their rifles at his chest. The Texans led General Santa Anna to a spreading live oak tree under which the tall man I had seen lose two horses sat with his wounded foot propped up and bandaged. I knew then that the man was, indeed, General Sam Houston, just as I had guessed.

A great argument arose among the Texan leaders. It was obvious that some of the Texans wanted to execute His Excellency for all the trouble he had caused, but General Houston apparently wanted him to be made a prisoner. General Houston won the argument, for His Excellency was made comfortable with food, water, and a smoke.

That night, I quietly climbed down the tree. I crept on hands and knees through the grass like a dog until I reached the bayou, slid into the river, and swam underwater to the other side. I saw campfires and heard the *norteamericanos* talking and laughing. The cool night air sent shivers through my body as I crawled from the water. Dashing from tree to tree, I worked my way through the woods and reached an open prairie filled with grasses and wildflowers. I stooped low and ran as fast as my feet would carry me. Soon I no longer heard the voices.

I walked all that night and all the next day, stopping for food only once when I saw some eggs in a henhouse. I ate them raw. I drank some well water and continued, my mind dazed and disconnected. I did not feel the earth beneath my feet nor the sting of the nettles or briers or cactus needles that lodged in my tattered blue uniform.

As I stumbled along, I tried to think what the future held. If I managed to somehow rejoin the rest of the army, would I be called a coward for running away? Would I be labeled a deserter and shot? Or would I be put back into the ranks, given a musket, and sent onward to battle again?

That night I slept in a pile of hay in a small barn near a burnt-out log house. I found a bag of corn that someone had hidden under a pail. I ate some of the hard, dry corn. The next morning I heard barking dogs, then voices. I jumped to my feet and peered between the crack of two logs. When I saw the familiar uniforms of Mexican soldiers, I sighed with relief. Never was I so happy to see the ugly face of Hector.

Hector shouted with glee and threw his dirty arms around me. He had received a flesh wound on the side of his cheek, and one finger was missing, but he was alive. I showed him the bag of corn. We ground it with rocks as best as we could and ate it raw.

Hector scrounged in the barn and found a pitchfork with only one tine.

"This will make a good weapon," he crowed. "I will stick the next rebel pig I see in the woods, and we will feast on pork."

We laughed, and it felt strange in my throat.

Our little group continued to move all day and night, only sleeping an hour at a time. Hector's pitchfork speared two fish and a rabbit. The food was meager, but it kept us alive. We did not talk much, but when we did, the topic always turned to the fate of His Excellency and the Mexican army.

"I do not understand why we have not passed the Mexican army marching east," I complained. "They were camped at the Brazos when I left them."

"General Filisola will avenge us," Hector said. "We still have four thousand troops in Texas. The enemy only has a thousand or so. We can easily defeat them."

"I do not know about General Filisola; after all, he is Italian," another soldier said. "But surely General Urrea will avenge the slaughter as soon as he learns of it. He has won every battle in this campaign. It is he who should have been made second-in-command."

"We have many cannons and howitzers," I added. "The enemy has only two little cannons."

"And we have a cavalry," Hector reminded them. "They are still at Gonzales under the command of General Andrade. The horses were so exhausted and thin from the long march, they had to rest. But by now they have eaten spring grass and should be in good shape."

We all agreed that the Mexican army, though separated into three parts, would soon regroup and attack the rebels with a vengeance. Our generals would not allow the deaths of our comrades to be in vain. I expected to see the army anytime and guessed that I would be given a new musket and shoes and rations and be sent back into the war.

On the third day, we met a small band of weary soldiers walking toward us from the direction of the Brazos River. They told us that the river was too wide and deep to cross and that there was no bridge or barge. Most of the Mexican soldiers who had escaped from San Jacinto were camped there now, unable to get across. Even the strongest swimmer was afraid to brave the torrent. This small group had decided to turn around and go back to surrender to the rebels, knowing they could not find food enough to survive. The news struck me like a blow in the guts.

"If there is no barge, then how did the Mexican army cross?" I asked.

"Yes, where is the army?" Hector demanded.

The stragglers all snorted and laughed. "The Mexican army did not cross the river. The Mexican army is retreating."

"Retreating!" Hector roared. "How can that be possible? By whose orders?"

"By the orders of General Santa Anna. Didn't you hear? He made terms of surrender with General Houston. In exchange for his life, he ordered the Mexican army to leave Texas."

"No," I shouted. "We cannot retreat. Our honor is at stake."

"It was only one battle!" Hector bellowed. "*¡Dios mío!* We were winning the war. You cannot give up the war because of one lost battle. The rebels threw everything they had at us and are weak, tired, and unfit for another grand battle. Now is the time to strike!" He plunged the point of the pitchfork into the muddy earth for emphasis.

The raggedy soldiers looked at Hector. "Perhaps you should tell your ideas to the generals," they joked. "Every soldier in camp agrees with you, but we have no say in this war. If we had, we would not have marched hundreds of leagues with no grass for the pack animals and no food for ourselves. We would not have massacred unarmed prisoners."

"The generals are fools," Hector said in disgust, and spat at the ground.

I looked around me. Every man's face was full of indignation and shame at the idea of retreating from an enemy who had been running for his life until only a few days ago.

We reached the Brazos River after dark. The campfires of the Mexican army twinkled on the other side, and I could hear the swift, deep water below. It was too dangerous to cross at night.

The next morning I said good-bye to Hector, who could not swim, and slid into the water. The current tugged at my legs mercilessly, and I felt myself being dragged downstream. Logs and debris passed by, tearing at my arms and legs. But at last I crawled ashore, safely on the other side.

I walked into the army encampment and sat on a stump. I removed my coatee and wrung it out and shook it in the warm sun. I heard arguing inside the nearest tent, then saw three generals emerge, their faces pale and filled with shock.

One turned to the other. "Well, it is over. We should have struck while we had the chance. El Presidente has lost Texas."

The other general buttoned his uniform, adjusted his bi-corn hat with its red, white, and green feathers, then squared his shoulders. "Now maybe the rest of Mexico will see what we have known all along—Santa Anna is insane."

Deep despair swept over me. I sank back onto the stump and held my head in my hands. I heard the tent flap rustle and saw General Urrea exit. Our eyes met a moment. I am sure I saw tears before the general turned away. All the victories he had fought so dearly for were now cast aside. Officers gathered around him, urging him to take charge of the army and attack the rebels in spite of Santa Anna's orders. But the general shook his head.

"I cannot disobey the orders of El Presidente," was all he said before returning to his division.

I replaced my damp clothes and looked across the river at Hector and the others. They would have to decide if they would swim the river, wait for it to subside, or surrender to the enemy, who would soon be coming this way.

I walked through the camp in a daze. I did not know who to report to: My sergeant was dead; my captain was dead; my colonel was dead; my general was a prisoner. As the word spread of His Excellency's orders, the army began packing up. Sutlers threw supplies in the river—barrels of whiskey and the food that had been so stingily rationed during our march. Now it was considered too heavy to carry. Wagons, boxes, all were abandoned. Houses filled with loot taken from the colonists were set afire. Knapsacks, saddles, things of immense value, were carelessly tossed into the fire or the river, while common soldiers with nothing were told to begin the retreat.

When some women found out that I had taken part in the battle at San Jacinto, they barraged me with questions about their loved ones. "Did you see my husband? Is my brother alive? Do you know what happened to my son?" I answered all the questions I could, but there was little hope for them. They wept and shrieked when I told them how the soldiers' bodies were left for the buzzards. I immediately regretted saying it, but my curse of honesty made me tell all.

I searched for Catalina, but she was not to be found. No one had seen her in days and no one knew her fate. It made my return all the more painful. Had I been too harsh with her? Had my words forced her to return to San Antonio de Béxar, or worse, to throw herself in the river?

Suddenly, I regretted every harsh word I had said to

her. I wished I had forgiven her and held her close and told her I loved her. For after so much death, what she had done seemed unimportant. And I knew now that I did love Catalina Sandoval, the goatherd. I loved her more than anything on this blood-filled earth.

TWENTY-THREE

Home

On April 28, one week after the fateful battle at the San Jacinto River, I fell in step with the remnants of the Guanajuato regiment on our retreat. We had no knapsacks, no shoes, no weapons. We were the marching dead. Each man's heart bled with shame. Each day that passed, we grew more gaunt and raggedy. What little clothing we had, had turned to faded, colorless rags.

Other units joined us on the long retreat, the cavalry from Gonzales, Sesma's troops from the north. All walked like skeletons with no hearts. We did not speak. We did not walk side by side like true soldiers, but in single file, each man deep in his own thoughts. We were not an army moving in unison, but four thousand separate ghosts.

The days turned into weeks as the disorganized and demoralized army trudged southward toward Río Bravo.

The heat increased, breathing down our backs like a fiery monster. Disease spread. Men, women, and children dropped by the wayside.

As we passed through the rich, fertile lands of southern Texas, where palm trees and tropical flowers swayed in the wind, I felt the bitter gall of disappointment and betrayal swell in my throat. Before the campaign I knew nothing of Texas and would not have cared if it were lost. But having seen its wealth and beauty, now I only felt regret. But mostly I felt hatred for the general who had given away this paradise.

It was with mixed feelings of pride and shame, of relief and regret, that I finally crossed the Río Bravo and left Texas behind. We arrived at Matamoros, a town swollen many times over with the presence of the army. Here we were regrouped and assigned to new battalions and given new orders.

It took several months for my regiment to reach the *presidio* at San Luis Potosí. It was October when I once again saw the narrow streets where the balconies almost touched. I thought about Esteban laughing at Catalina chasing her goats down the street. I thought about Señor Sandoval sipping his coffee and telling stories about the Revolution. I thought about Sergeant Ildefonso, who found love so late in life. And my dear sisters. All were gone now, all sacrificed for the vainglory of a foolish general.

The Mexican government was almost bankrupt because of the Texas campaign. Soldiers were chosen for early discharge—some very old, some very young, some severely crippled.

One day in December I was called to the commander's quarters.

"Are you Lorenzo Bonifacio of Guanajuato state, village of San Javier?" the captain asked me.

"Yes, sir," I replied, a strange feeling creeping over me.

"Today is a fortunate day for you, Private Bonifacio," he said, not bothering to look up from the stack of papers on his desk. "You are being given a full honorable discharge from the Mexican army."

"Me? But why, sir?" I asked in amazement.

The commander took a small scribbled note in his hand, then looked up.

"Apparently you have a friend in high command," he said, smiling. "Someone who cares about your future as a flute player. This note was attached to your military records. A note from General Santa Anna himself."

"But—but I did nothing honorable. I only played my flute."

The commander scowled. "Are you refusing this special discharge? Do you want to remain in the army nine more years? I can oblige you."

"No, sir. I am not refusing, but I don't understand—"

"Just be thankful and don't argue. Take the discharge and get out of here. You are the most fortunate private I have ever seen."

I accepted a few *pesos* for my pay. I was also given a small cheap honor badge to show that I had served in the Texas campaign. I did not bother to put it on my collar. I did not look back as I passed the citadel where soldiers were sleeping, where I had first fired a musket and dreamed of glorious battles. I pulled my hat low over my head and headed toward the hills.

■ ■ ■

When I reached my little village, the sun had not yet risen. As I walked to my *adobe* house, I was surprised to see a light in the window and hear the cry of a baby. I saw the shadow of a woman moving across the doorway. She rocked a cradle and sang to the baby in a sweet, pure voice. I entered the door and stopped.

"Aunt Florencia!" I gasped.

For a moment she stared, her lips slightly parted in shock, her chin starting to tremble. Then she opened her arms wide and wrapped them around me. She sobbed and shook with emotion, and I could not hold back my own tears. We clung to each other for a full moment before separating.

"I thought you were killed at San Jacinto," she said, her voice shaking. "The messengers said that all of the Aldama company was slaughtered; all of the Toluca was killed; that everyone else was taken prisoner. I could not bear to stay in Texas another day." She took a handkerchief from her pocket and wiped her nose.

The newborn infant made a noise, and we both turned and looked at it in its cradle, its small fists wiggling.

"I named him Hernando, after his father. He would be very happy to have a son."

"This is your child?" I asked in shock.

"*Sí.* My child." Aunt Florencia lifted the baby from the crib and sat down across from me. "Do you not recognize the face on this child?" she asked. "Look closely." She jostled the plump baby on her knee, and it smiled a toothless grin. A deep dimple spread on the left cheek.

"Sergeant Ildefonso?"

Aunt Florencia smiled. "*Sí.* We were married only one night. It is a miracle, is it not?"

I touched the baby's petal-soft skin. Suddenly everything about the child looked like the good sergeant. I laughed and threw my hat into the air.

"Yes, it is a miracle, Aunt Florencia. Out of war and death has come love and life." I took the child into my arms and felt its warmth and softness. It grasped my finger and cooed.

I heard a man coughing in the bed in the other room. A question creased my brow. "A man is sleeping here?" I asked, as I put the baby down.

"*Sí,* a very wonderful man," Aunt Florencia replied, and smiled. "You must come meet him."

My face turned hot. "How could you, Aunt Florencia? So soon after the sergeant died. You are still in widow's weeds, are you not?"

"Florencia, who is it?" a man's voice asked, and a tall form filled the doorframe. I recognized him instantly as the soldier who had put the good sergeant out of his misery and seen to his burial.

"You?" I said in disbelief. "You are living here?"

"And why not? It is my house."

A flash of anger rushed over me. "No, *señor.* It is not your house. It is mine. And I must ask you to leave."

The man's mouth dropped slightly, then he looked at my aunt. She was smiling and nodding, her eyes wet with tears. *"Sí, sí,"* she said, as if they were speaking some kind of code.

"Lorenzo! My son!" The man surged forward and wrapped his arms around me. He smelled of corn and tobacco and the sweat of a hardworking man. When the truth hit me, I began shaking all over. My heart pounded in my chest and my breath came short. Tears filled my eyes and spilled down my cheeks.

"Papa! Papa!" was all I could say. "I looked for you every day. You were there all along. All along."

The man pulled away, his own eyes red and wet, his chin quivering. "The moment I saw you, I felt like I had known you before. It was only when I saw my dear sister, Florencia, weeping at the graveside of the sergeant, that I learned you were a soldier in the army. I looked for you, but never saw you again. I was sent to the north with Ramírez y Sesma. You were sent to follow Santa Anna. *Gracias a Dios,* you survived the carnage at San Jacinto."

Aunt Florencia began cooking a grand breakfast for me. She told me to go to my old bed and sleep, but I was restless. I got up from my straw mat and climbed to the top of the hill where I loved so dearly to watch the sun rise over the distant *sierras*. How many times had I dreamed of this place while I was tramping over deserts and mountains and crossing raging rivers? Slowly, I breathed in the fragrance of juniper needles. Below, the grasses had turned golden as the winter moved in. The cornfields were fallow and corn glistened on rooftops. It was December. I had been away for over a year. It seemed like a hundred.

From my leather pouch, I removed the note that General Santa Anna had written. It had gone through rains and river crossings inside the little bag, and though its ink was now smeared and faded, the words were still legible. I closed my eyes and could clearly see Esteban's smiling face as he read it aloud: "Lorenzo Bonifacio and friend are requested to come to my tent. Presidente-General Antonio López de Santa Anna."

Suddenly I heard the bleating of goats and turned to see a small herd frolicking near the bottom of the hill.

"I see you have returned," a voice said behind me. I spun around and saw Catalina sitting on a rock, her striped *rebozo* wrapped around her sturdy shoulders. Her dark eyes twinkled in her face, which was once again plump and darkened by a long summer of sun.

"Yes, I have returned," I replied softly, trying to hide

my delight that she was still alive. "I see you are in the business of raising goats again."

She shrugged. "I took your words of advice and did not wait for that officer. They told us no one survived San Jacinto, so I had no reason to stay in Texas, did I? I found some goats in the fields. *Norteamericano* goats, but goats nevertheless. They reminded me of why I was put on Earth."

I smiled. "It is good to see that you survived, Catalina."

"I am surprised that you are back here. Didn't you tell me once that you hated this village and wanted to see the world?" She climbed the little hill and stood in front of me, her stocky body swathed in layers of cotton and wool. The odor of cornmeal and goats and red chiles clung to her like an exotic perfume. "Why did you come back here, Lorenzo?"

I looked at her, then at the goats, the fields, the mountains, the valleys, the sky.

"Because I have decided I like the smell of goats more than the smell of gunpowder."

Catalina laughed, then nodded toward the note in my hand. "What is that? Something important?"

I glanced at the note a final time, then crumpled it up and tossed it to the goats, who quickly ripped it apart and ate it.

"No, it is nothing of importance," I said. "Nothing at all."

GLOSSARY
OF SPANISH WORDS

abuelito—grandfather

adiós—good-bye

adobe—a building material made of mud and dried in the sun

agave—century plant

alcalde—leader of a town, similar to mayor

almuerzo—a meal in late morning

amigo—friend

anglo—an English-speaking American

arroyo—creek bed

avemaría—Ave María; a prayer asking for help from Mary, mother of Jesus

barranco—a small ravine

buenas noches—good night

bueno—good

buenos días—good day

buñuelo—a flat pastry

calabozo—a jail cell

caldo—soup

camposanto—cemetery near a church

cantina—a tavern

caporal—corporal

¡caramba!—darn; a mild curse

carreta—a cart with two large wheels, often pulled by oxen

casa grande—the main house on a ranch or *hacienda*

castañetas—castanets; musical instrument held in the hand to make clicks

cigarrillo—cigarette

comal—a large, flat pan or stone on which *tortillas* are cooked

la comida—the midday meal, usually eaten around one or two o'clock

compadre—companion, buddy

criollo—a person born in Mexico, but whose parents were Spanish

curendera—a healer who uses herbs and religious ceremonies to cure the sick

de nada—it's nothing; no bother

degüello—a tune played by military trumpets signifying no mercy

El Despoblado—a sparsely inhabited region of northern Mexico and western Texas marked by rugged mountains and deserts

día de los muertos—Day of the Dead; a festival held on November 1 and 2, to honor deceased loved ones

el diablo—the devil

¡Dios mío!—My God; my goodness

don—title of honor given to wealthy men
doña—title of honor given to wealthy women
Doña Blanca—a children's song and game

eh bien—well, then
excelente—excellent

fandango—a fast-paced Spanish dance; also a dance party or ball
fiesta—festival
¡Firmes!—Attention!
frijoles—beans
¡Fuego!—Fire!

gracias—thank you
gracias a Dios—thank God; thank goodness
guano—manure, especially that derived from birds or bats
guitarra—guitar

hacienda—a large ranch that raises cattle or horses
herraderos—the annual roundup and branding of cattle, accompanied by parties and display of the talents of cowboys

¡Idiotos!—Idiots!
indios—Native Americans

jacales—small huts constructed of poles and sticks

lépero—an uncouth, foulmouthed, gross person
la leva—a method of conscripting soldiers into the army

¡Listos!—Get ready!

¡Madre mía!—Goodness gracious!

maguey—a plant in the agave family, with fleshy leaves and a sap used to make a strong alcoholic beverage called *pulque*

mal de ojo—evil eye; a spell cast on a child causing bad luck and sickness

mamacita—Mommy

manga—a type of cape

masa—a mixture of finely ground corn from which *tortillas* are made

mestizo—a person who is half Spanish and half Indian

metate—a stone tool on which corn is ground

muchacho—boy

muchas gracias—thank you very much

muy bien—very well

muy bueno—very good

niñas—little girls

norteamericano—North American, especially one from the United States

¡Olé!—Bravo! Good job!; a shout given at bullfights

padre—father; title used by Catholic priests

pan dulce—sweet bread; a Mexican pastry

patatas—potatoes

peón—a common laborer on a farm or ranch

peso—a unit of Mexican money

petate—a straw sleeping mat that can be rolled up

piloncillo—a cylinder of raw sugar

piñata—a decorated container filled with treats like nuts and candy, hung with a rope, and broken open by children at festivals and parties

pinole—flour made of various grains

pistola—pistol

por favor—please

la posada—a religious procession before Christmas that reenacts Joseph and Mary's search for a place to stay before the birth of Jesus

El Presidente Mr. President

presidio—a military fort, often located near a mission

¡pronto!—quick!

prostituta—prostitute

pulque—a strong alcoholic drink made from the sap of *maguey* plants

¡Qué diablos!—What the devil!

quinceañera—a girl's fifteenth birthday celebration

ranchero—rancher

rancho—ranch

real, reales—a unit of Spanish money

rebozo—a woman's decorative blanket used as a shawl; also to carry babies

república—a republic

río—river

sarape—a decorative man's blanket carried around the shoulders

sargento—sergeant

señor—Mr.; sir

señora—Mrs.; lady

señorita—Miss; girl or young woman

shako—a tall, stiff military cap, often decorated with feathers

sí—yes

sierra—a jagged mountain range

siesta—a resting period after the main meal of the day, around three o'clock

¡Silencio!—Be quiet!

soldaderas—civilians who followed the army, mostly women and children

soldado—soldier

¡El stupido!—stupid

tejano—a Mexican person living in Texas

teniente—lieutenant

tierra caliente—the hot, tropical regions of southern Mexico

toque de silencio—a drum or bugle signal, calling men to retire for the night

tortilla—a flat circle of bread made with corn flour

vaquero—cowboy; horse-riding man who takes care of cattle on a *hacienda*

vara—a Spanish measurement equivalent to approximately one yard

¡Viva!—Long live!

El Volcán—the volcano; nickname given to one of the Mexican cannons